F.A.H
LIVES

STORIES
AND
THOUGHTS

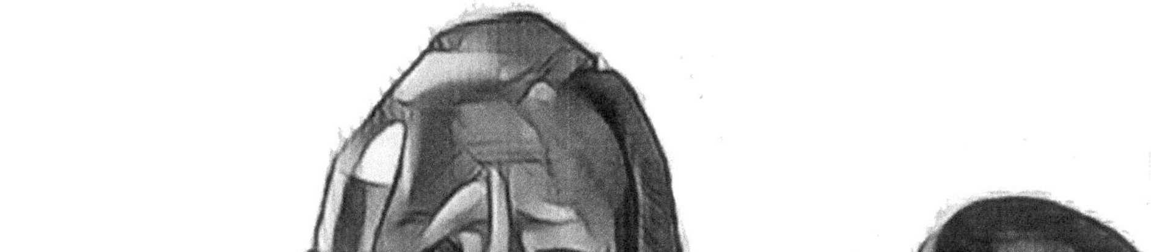

1st Edition. October 27, 2023.

Paperback ISBN# 978-1-7370337-7-6

Ebook ISBN: 978-1-7370337-8-3

Ilustrations by Ethan Adorno & Alland Adorno

Written by F.A.H.

Edited by Luz I. Ruiz, PhD

CONTENTS

DEDICATION

T HIS BOOK IS DEDICATED to mis viejos[1], in the order they have left me: Fortuna, Teresa, Pedro, Ismael, Felix, and Antonia. Without their stories, there would not be mine and there would be none of these that I have written.

For my mom, Marina, the only one I have left...

Because of my elders, I share this thought:

"I walk in the footsteps of mis viejos. If I do not reach paradise that way, it is because that place does not exist."

---

1. Viejos: Elders

FOREWORD

THE STORIES AND THOUGHTS in this book, woven together, are not confined to the realm of a singular perspective. They traverse and encompass the spectrum of both the ordinary and the mystical. I have purposefully abstained from imposing a common theme upon these narratives, for I refuse to be limited by the confines of a predefined box. My aim is simply to give voice to the diverse experiences that countless individuals have encountered throughout their lives. It is with this intention that I present to you: *LIVES: Stories and Thoughts.*

Within the *"Stories"* section, you will find a collection of narratives that delve into the tapestry of everyday life and explore the enchanting occurrences that form part of the myths in my homeland, Puerto Rico. These tales touch upon topics deeply intertwined with familial bonds and significant events that have shaped the popular beliefs of our community.

As for the *"Thoughts"* section, it serves as a heartfelt dedication to my cherished loved ones and an avenue to express the profound emotions that have arisen from the inevitable experience of loss.

I harbor no grand aspirations of emulating the literary prowess of Gabriel García Márquez or Enrique Laguerre. Instead, my sole aspiration is to embrace my own voice, identified by the initials F.A.H. It is my sincere hope that this unique perspective will suffice to captivate and inspire you as you embark upon the exploration of these *Stories and Thoughts.*

Stories

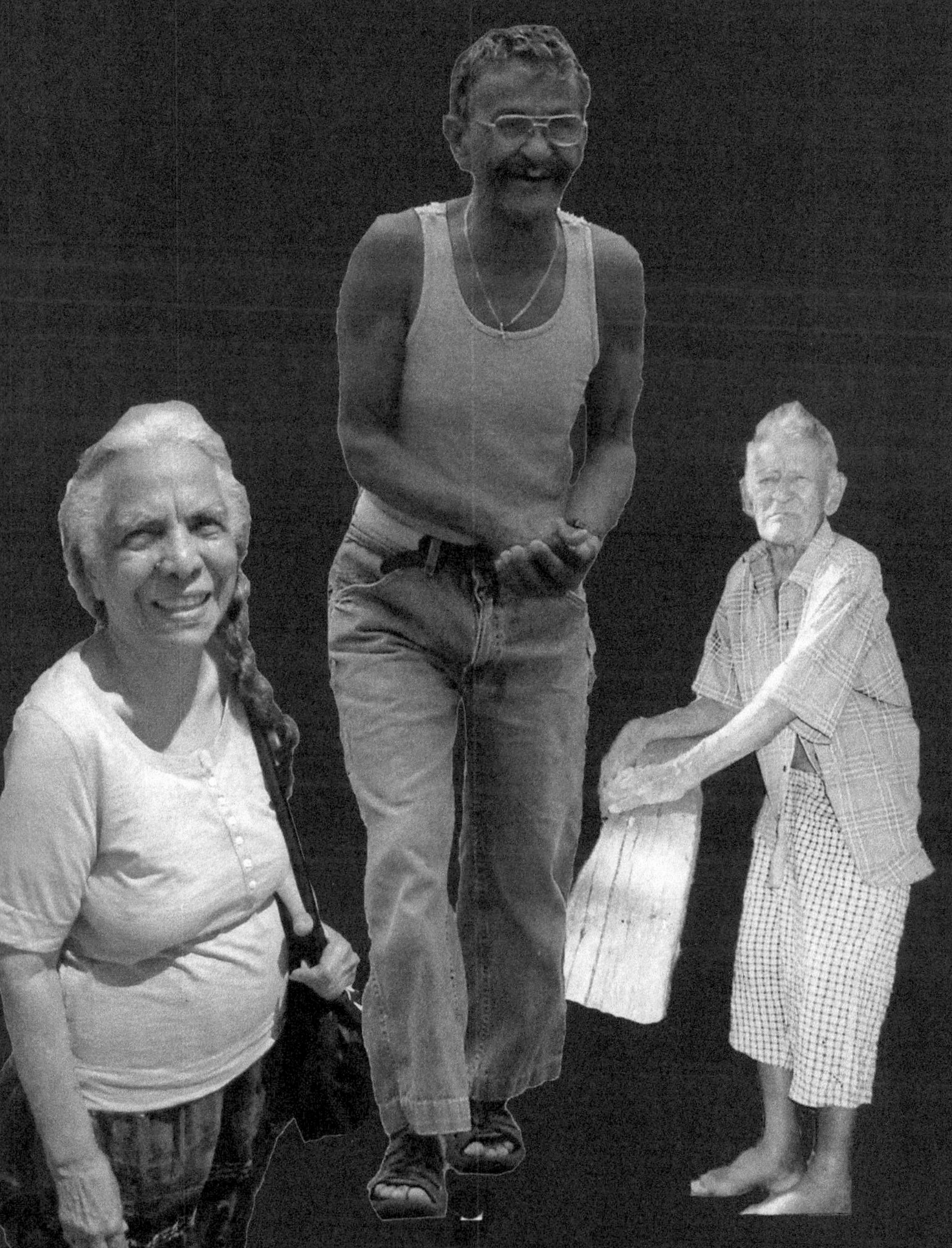

THE FOREIGNER

I T WAS A HOT and humid summer morning, the same as all other mornings on a tropical island like Puerto Rico, when Antonio returned to the place where he took his first steps. The sun shone on the blue sky and a breeze air ran around cooling the surroundings in a defiant challenge to the burning star. Around this place, animals sought shelter from the heat and people hid under sombrillas[1] or balcones[2] to protect their skin from the burning sensation of the sun's rays. Flying higher than the plane that brought him back to his childhood barrio[3], was the excitement inside his chest combined with the emotional cravings in his soul, stunned by so many years of absence. The opportunity to see his people again and reminiscence about his childhood and youth stirred up in Antonio great happiness. He looked forward to talking about the past with them, re-membering his humble beginnings and his mistakes as a child. He eagerly awaited asking them about what virtues, if any, they observed in him. He wanted to reunite and talk to all his Viejos[4], and there were many because in a neighborhood as small as this one everyone knew each other in an intimate way. Antonio's childhood dreams were trapped in that place where he had had his first steps, his first stumbles. The image of this place lived frozen in time in the mind of this old man who had left many years

---

1. Sombrillas: umbrellas

2. Balcones: balconies

3. Barrio: neighborhood

4. Viejos: elders.

ago in search of better economic opportunities in life. For these reasons and more, Antonio searched and searched around for all his people, but he only spotted strangers, and they in turn only saw a foreigner.

He arrived at his mother's home, a woman who was already advanced in age. He greeted her and spent some time discussing his arrival details and plans for the following days. Thereafter, he went out to take a stroll around the neighborhood to see his friends, but all he could find were strangers. Some of them turned around to look at him without uttering a word; some of them did not even bother to take their gazes off their cell phones to observe the foreigner who walked amongst them. Antonio felt weird, and out of place. Nevertheless, he continued his walk through the barrio on his way to visit one of his childhood friends. As he approached the porch, of his friend's house, he called out his name:

"Ramón..." -Antonio called, but no one answered.

"Ramón." -he repeated after a few seconds.

"Who is it?" -asked an unknown voice from inside the house.

"I am Antonio, Don Ignacio's son. The one that moved to New York in the 1980s.

After a few seconds, a woman appeared at the door looking puzzled and confused. She looked at him sternly before asking:

"You're one of <u>el difunto</u>[5] Don Ignacio's sons?"

"Yes, I'm the one who emigrated to the United States when I was younger."

"And you're looking for Ramon Mendéz, right?"

"Yes, yes Ramón, the one who lives in this house. I just want to say Hi."

"Well, <u>si lo ves cogele miedo</u>[6], Ramón died two years ago."

"OH, I'm so sorry. I didn't know anything about it."

"It's ok, no harm done."

---

5. El difunto: the deceased.

6. sí lo ves cogele miedo: if you see him be afraid.

"I'm terribly sorry. My dad used to keep me in the loop about these things, and I lost him a long time ago."

"I know Don Ignacio was one of the good ones."

"May I ask, how did Ramón die?"

"He was cancer-stricken, but he didn't know until it was too late. You know how stubborn you guys can be. He refused to see a doctor until he couldn't take it anymore. By then it was too late, and the illness had spread through his body."

"What a shame, Ramón was an incredibly good person."

"I'm Ramón's youngest daughter Inés, the one who inherited the house when he passed."

"Well, I would say it's a pleasure to meet you, but under the circumstances, I just want to say I'm sorry for your loss."

"Thank you, it's nice to have people who care about our loved ones."

"Well, let me go now to see who else I can greet before I leave."

"Take care and say hello to your mother on my behalf."

Antonio resumed his walk around the barrio, this time with a heavy heart upon learning about the passing of his childhood companion, a few years ago. The loss of this dear friend, during his absence from the Island, brought him back to the time when he, too, lost his father. His viejo, Don Ignacio, died many years back during a chilly winter day, while Antonio was chasing his "American Dream" of prosperity. Memories of moments apart from his father, while he was on his pilgrimage searching for a better life for himself, and his family, also came rushing in to remind him about the valuable lessons he taught him. The son remembered when his father said to him:

"Be caring and respectful to others and appreciate what you have; be decent and honest, and work hard for what you want and need." These prized lessons were planted so deep into his consciousness that not even the passing of many years could uproot any single one of them. He used these lessons to guide his life and had tried to pass them on to his own children. Though, among all these recollections was the most painful one , the day he received the phone call informing him of his orphanhood. Antonio felt a twinge in his heart. The same pain he experienced hearing his uncle's broken voice on the other end of the phone telling him about his father's

passing, while at the same time hearing his mother screaming hysterically in the background. These images caused him to think about all the stored pain and emptiness trapped in time, and to reflect about the nostalgia one tends to feel when returning to a place looking for something that is no longer there.

Soon after these moments of painful memories and empty feelings, Antonio continued his way to gaze upon the places he held dear in his heart. For instance, Doña Fela's house was no longer there, in its place were only broken walls semi-covered with bushes. Neither was Don Tómas' grocery store. In the location where this grocery store once stood, now was una barra de mala muerte[7] . Antonio looked and looked and all he could see were shadows around him. The shadows of all the people who had died through time and its lethargic movements. Don Aguedo's and Doña María's house did not seem the same. Also missing were Doña Candelaria and Doña Ernesta, two elderly women who had been part of his youth and who offered him their wisdom and advice more than once. Yet from this place he missed his abuelo[8] , Pello, the most. He, too, had passed on during Antonio's long journey to the States. In the plot of land where his grandfather's house once upon a time stood, there was NOTHING, not even a wall on which he would have loved to lean on to remember the stories his abuelo told him, long before he left this place in search of a more convenient future. Antonio felt strange as his mind tried to balance the reality of the moment, with the memories he had saved all his life. Then he realized that this place, which he had jealously guarded in his heart through all those years, was as real as a unicorn. All these things made Antonio feel like a stranger in his own home. So, he cut his tour short and went back to his mother's house feeling disappointed. When he entered the house, he found his mom in the kitchen and immediately asked a question:

"Mam[9] í, why didn't you tell me that Ramón had died?"

"I didn't tell you? Are you sure? I believe that I did a couple of years ago." -answered the woman with her sights still on the stove.

"You told me two years ago, a la verdad[10] that I don't remember."

---

7. una barra de mala muerte: a dangerous or dubios bar.

8. Abuelo: grandfather

9. Mami: slang for "mom".

10. A la verdad: to tell you the truth.

"You don't remember but I did tell you."

"Well, I went to his house looking for him like a zangano[11]."

"Inés his younger daughter lives there now. She took care of him when he got sick."

"I know, she told me about it."

"Who else did you visit?"

"No one else, I went to see the sites but didn't feel like going to anymore homes."

"Why not?"

"Because it seems to me that everyone I knew, is already dead."

"Well, time stands still for no one."

"It feels weird, nonetheless."

"Did you go to visit Filomena?"

"Is Filomena still alive? Wow! I didn't expect that."

"Well, she is still among the living, a little senile like many people her age, but healthy, nonetheless."

"Caramba! I must go and see her then."

"Yes, you should! Right after you eat the <u>arroz con gandulez[12]</u> that I cooked for you."

After eating his mother's food, Antonio left his home a little happier than before on his way to Filomena's home. She was another elderly woman whom he had known since childhood, because she was one of his father's best friends. Once again, he found himself amid another set of strangers that looked at him like he was a puzzle piece that didn't fit, even if they already knew who he was, because in a place so small like this one nothing happens by chance without the locals finding out about it almost im-

---

11. Zangano: dumb person.

12. Arroz con gandulez: local food: yellow rice cooked mixed with pigeon peas.

mediately, and Antonio was aware of that fact. He was walking towards Filomena's home when a total stranger approached him amicably:

"Cousin Toño[13]*, cuando carajo*[14] *you get here?"* -asked the man with a big smile on his lips and whose voice Antonio recognized immediately.

"Cousin Juan, what a pleasure to see you!" -Antonio lunged at the man to give him a heartfelt hug.

"So, tell me, tell me when did you get here?"

"Last night."

"For how long are you staying?"

"Two weeks."

"Two weeks na'ma[15] *."*

"Yes man, only two weeks."

"Did you go around to see people?"

"¡Ay bendito![16] *What people? It seems like everyone I know has died."*

"Everyone except for me, I'm still vivito y coleando[17] *."*

"I see that, although, I almost didn't recognize you."

"Well, you never call anyone, how would you know who is alive or dead?"

"I know, I know! Believe me that I regret that now."

"And where are you going right now?"

"To Filomena's house. I still cannot believe that she's alive."

---

13. Toño: Nickname for Antonio

14. Cuando carajo: when the hell

15. Na'ma: slang for "only that"

16. ¡Ay bendito!: Slang that expresses happiness, sadness, or surprise depending on the tonality of the voice

17. vivito y coleando: A saying for alive and well.

"That condena[18] is so old, but she's still alive and kicking."

"That's what mamí told me. I couldn't believe it."

"And how is titi[19] Agustina? I haven't seen her in a while."

"She's doing fine, you know with achaques[20] , but well."

"We all have achaques now."

"I know, getting old is not fun."

"Toño, come by my house later so we can continue talking."

"Ok, Juan, I will see you later."

"Later then."

The two said goodbye and Antonio thought, *"gosh not even cousin Juan seems familiar to me"*. He continued walking while analyzing how time had caused havoc in the physical appearance of the people he knew, and for a moment he thought about how old he had gotten himself. His youth had escaped him while living his foreigner's life still looking for that better life for which he was searching. Antonio concluded that he was not exempted from the claws of time. He had left the place young and full of dreams and now he had returned full of the nightmares that despair causes. It didn't matter how hard he tried; he couldn't reconcile the Puerto Rico of his dreams with that of the present. When he arrived at Filomena's house, he stood outside and called out:

"Mena[21] !"

"Who is there?" -answered a tired voice from inside the house.

"Is me Antonio, Don Ignacio's son."

"El difunto Don Ignacio's son, which one?"

---

18. Condená: term of endearment

19. Titi: auntie

20. Achaques: slang for persistent pains.

21. Mena: nickname for Filomena

"Antonio, although you used to call me Toñito."

"Toñito mijo[22] when did you return? Come in, come in, and give me a hug."

Antonio crossed the threshold of the door, and the old woman was already walking slowly towards him. She embraced him immediately and Antonio felt shaken by that display of human warmth, which he had been looking for on his return trip. And wrapped momentarily in the arms of that old lady who had been one of the integral figures of his childhood, he felt alive for a couple of seconds. Filomena was one of his deceased father's closest friends and he had always seen her as part of his family. While she was embracing him, he thought of his dad, Ignacio, and for a moment imagined that he was hugging him, instead of the old woman. Antonio felt like crying. It was an attack of the present, mixed with the past, which twisted the body of the man who had left young, full of dreams, and now returned old, full of anguish and regrets. In his search for a better life, he had lost many important people, his grandparents, his uncles, some cousins, and friends, and above all his father. He came back carrying the eternal emptiness left by loss and tried to hold back tears, while coming loose from the wise woman's loving embrace.

"I came yesterday." -said Antonio answering the question Filomena had asked before hugging him.

"How long are you staying?" -she asked looking directly into his eyes.

"Two weeks."

"Did you bring your family, or did you come alone?"

"I came alone, they couldn't come because they're all working already."

"Do you have any nietos[23]?"

"I have two, a boy and a girl."

"How old are they?"

"The boy is five and the girl is eight."

"Ok, and how are you doing?"

---

22. Mijo: slang for "my son".

23. Nietos: grandchildren

"I'm doing fine." -Antonio answered looking down at the floor trying to hide from Filomena's gaze.

"If you are fine, why the long face?"

"What long face?"

"That long face! You cannot deceive me. I have known you since before you were born and I know something is eating at you. Also, I <u>estoy vieja pero no ciega</u>[24] ."

"I don't know what to say."

Filomena looked at him for a couple of seconds trying to adjust her tone of voice, cautious about what she would say next. She was on to something, and he knew it. She was not lying when she said she had known Antonio since before he had taken his first breath of air in this world. For that reason, she remained quiet, giving him the opportunity to decide if he was going to tell her the truth or lie to her face. Antonio looked at her as she waited for his answer; then, he decided to let his soul guide his words:

"I feel very strange and I don't know why. I know that I should be happy to be here, but a feeling of emptiness is overwhelming me."

"So, you're feeling sad and lost?"

"Something like that. I don't know how to explain it. I just feel like I don't know anyone anymore."

"Well, that's normal mijo. Remember that time stands still for no one."

"I know, I know, but I had not felt like that since..."

As he paused, Antonio's mind traveled to the past to visit memories that were hidden deep inside his soul. Now, they had suddenly returned. He recalled that day at the airport when his father hugged him goodbye, before getting on the plane for his first trip as a Puerto Rican immigrant to the United States. He recalled the first time he experienced a double cold in his new country. First, the coldness of the atmosphere; and second, the coldness with which people treated each other. He recalled the calls to his parents over the years, and among these the call that had notified him of his grandfather's death. However, wrapped in all these sad memories were also many moments of joy shared with his grandfather, his parents, and

---

24. estoy vieja pero no ciega: I am old, but not blind.

his siblings despite the distance – like the anniversaries and birthdays and the celebrations of family milestones, etc. Suddenly, these thoughts were interrupted by Filomena's voice.

"What's wrong with you? ¿Te quedaste mudo?[25] *"*

"Oh! No, no forgive me I got distracted."

"Don't think too much about the things that cannot be changed."

"What are you saying?" -Antonio asked trying to hide behind the question.

"You're thinking about the past and no matter what you do, nothing will change."

"I know but..."

"-Mijo everyone dies and there's nothing we can do about it. The only thing we can do is to continue living." -interrupted Filomena.

"I know, but..."

"But nothing mijo, you're still alive and while that's the case you should enjoy it as much as possible."

"That's what I want to do."

"Then enjoy your trip and don't waste time thinking."

"Ok, I will."

"You must do that and don't leave without saying goodbye to me. Remember that estoy más vieja que Matuzalen[26] *, and I'm not going to live forever."*

"Don't say that; you know there is no way I would leave without saying bye."

Antonio left Filomena's house with a slightly relieved soul, for at least she was still there. He kept walking to go to his cousin Juan's house and once again observed that it was not only that people had changed, but the neighborhood had also changed. There were more houses than land, as

---

25. ¿Te quedastes mudo: did you go mute?

26. Estoy más vieja que Matuzalen: Local saying, I am older than matuzalen (Bible's oldest character.)

the beautiful landscapes he remembered as a young boy had disappeared forever. There were new paved roads and pathways than previously. It was evident that progress and time had taken away part of nature and people, respectively. A few minutes later he arrived at his cousin's house, and they had various conversations about the past and the present. Other relatives arrived and between hugs and greetings, they decided to play dominoes.

"Cousin, it seems like you haven't played dominoes in a while." -said his cousin named Pedro.

"It's been a while." -commented Antonio.

"The stores don't sell dominoes out there or there're no people to play with?"

"There're dominoes there; what we don't have is the time to play with family and friends."

"What do you mean there is no time?" -asked Pedro curiously.

"That's because there you spend most of your time on the train commuting to work or on the job."

"What kind of life is that?"

"Such is life out there."

"That's the reason I never moved out there. What for? To be cold and working all my life for someone else and not have time to do anything fun?"

"Working for other people is what we all do."

"Yeah! But in the United States, you work and work and never own anything. Your house is never yours and you pay taxes to the day you die."

"That's true, but in the States, you don't have to estar <u>lambiendo ojo</u>[27] to get a job like you do here, on the Island, where the opportunities you get depend on the people you know. All these politicos <u>come mierdas</u>[28] steal everything from everyone."

"I'll never leave my Island, no matter what."

---

27. estar lambiendo ojo: local saying that translates to kissing ass.

28. Politicos comemierdas: Cocksucker politicians

"I left and I haven't had any regrets. -replied Antonio lying."

The conversation turned into a shouting debate between Antonio and his estranged relatives. After a few intense moments of shouting and reproaching, one person sitting at the table intervened and the game of dominoes continued. Then, they began to relax and behave as if nothing had happened. Because not even the long separation from those people, sharing a game of dominoes and habitual conversation, was enough to destroy the blood ties between them. After eating and drinking enough ron caña[29] , they said goodbye. As Antonio prepared to walk back to his mother's house, he turned to his cousin, Juan, and told him how grateful he was for the time spent together. Juan responded:

"Cousin Toño that's what the family is for, wait for me. I'll take you home."

"There's no need for that, I'm not that drunk. I can go home by myself." -Antonio replied.

"It's not a matter of you being drunk; it's that this place is not like the one you used to remember. No one knows you anymore, so it's dangerous for you to walk alone at this time of night."

"Is so bad here that you can't walk alone at night any longer?"

"You can, but you must know where to walk with all the <u>hijos de puta</u>[30] out there."

"Are you sure you're not exaggerating a little?"

"No, I'm not, and I'm not going to let you out of my sight at this hour. Titi Agustina will kill me if something happens to you."

"Ok, then take the tourist home." -replied Antonio with a little sarcasm in his voice.

"Don't play the pendejo[31] game with me, you know that I'm not lying."

"Ok, ok. Let's go then."

---

29. Ron caña: Puerto Rican moonshine

30. Hijos de puta: sons of bitches

31. Pendejo: asshole, dumb.

The two men walked under the starry night and continued to talk about their lives and everything that had changed. They finally arrived at their destination and said good night. Juan extended a new invitation to a second game night to his cousin before returning to his home, and Antonio gladly accepted. Antonio stood outside the house for a few minutes listening to the singing of the coquí[32] . It is a fact, that this melodious and familiar sound: coqui, coqui, coqui that cannot be heard anywhere else in the world. It is the endearing and unforgettable sound that every Puerto Rican knows so well. For a short while, he stopped feeling like a stranger in his own homeland and just tried to enjoy that living moment of peace and serenity. When he entered his house, his mother was already asleep. He stood at her bedroom door to look at her and realized how much time had passed since he said goodbye for the first time. This led him to think about the future and the real possibility of losing her in a few years. Only God knew how many times he had asked his mother to go live with him in New York, only to have her answer that she was fine at her own home. Besides, she did not like the long winters of Nuevayork[33] . The next morning, he woke up early and his mother was already in the kitchen, making coffee. He entered the kitchen, and his mother greeted him as usual:

"Good morning, mijo; <u>Dios te bendiga</u>[34] ". -she served him his breakfast and sat down to talk to him.

"Where were you yesterday?" -his mother asked while taking a sip of hot coffee.

"I went to see Filomena and to cousin Juan's house." -he replied.

"And how are the people?"

"As usual. We ate and played dominoes."

"And today, what are you going to do?"

"I'm thinking about going to the cemetery to visit the old man. Do you want to come with me?"

"No, I can't go there, I'm still unable to approach his grave."

---

32. Coquí: a species of frog that can only survive in Puerto Rico

33. Nuevayork: Puerto rican way of saying New York.

34. Dios te bendiga: may God bless you.

"That's ok, but I'm going. I must talk to him."

"Take something to clean the grave because none of your brothers do it."

"Ok. I will clean it myself. Are you sure you don't want to come with me?"

"Yes, I'm sure. When you go say hi for me."

"I will. Then let me get going."

The man boarded his rental car and headed to the cemetery where he had buried his father many years earlier. This trip caused him to remember the silent and sorrowful goodbye he had to give his father as he lay lifeless in his casket, the day of his funeral. How SORRY he was for not having been able to say goodbye to him while he was still alive. He thought about the words he never said to his father; he thought about the conversations he never had with the man who saw him grow up, and who taught him so much about life. Later, as Antonio drove towards the main entrance of the cemetery, there seemed to be an uneasy sensation in the air. He stopped the car for a moment, looked around in all directions and realized how dilapidated this place appeared to him today. It was no longer the sacred place that he imagined. It was as if the cemetery was also getting old.

He continued driving slowly along the small road leading toward his father's grave site, looking for a closer parking space. Antonio found himself momentarily lost. He looked around in all directions while trying to remember the exact location of his dad's tomb site. Painful memories of his viejo's death flashed by hunting him again. Images of his father lying inside the off-white casket surrounded by floral arrangements; the sensation of the heavy sense of sadness inside the funeral home; the sea of faces offering heartfelt condolences. The eternal pains of loss. Oh, how he regretted not visiting sooner to chat with the old man, and to bring him flowers. Eventually, he located his father's grave, and with a heavy heart realized that no one seemed to have visited that spot for a long, long time. Antonio opened the car's trunk and took out some tools and flowers that he had bought on the way there. He walked to the grave and knelt to begin the process of pulling out weeds and cleaning all debris around Ignacio's resting place. While cleaning he experienced feelings of disappointment and sadness. How was it that his brothers didn't have time to keep their father's resting place clean? He felt that they were so ungrateful and disrespectful to the man's memory. When Antonio finished cleaning the grave, he placed flowers on top of the headstone, sat down and began to talk:

"Old man, is me Antonio, I came to see you and I would like to talk to you. I don't know if you could hear me, but I must tell you that I love you and that I

will never, ever forget you. papí[35], I'm so sorry I didn't spend more time with you. I was young, full of ambition, and ignorant. I didn't have the wisdom to realize how much you meant to me while I still had you in my life. I missed so many moments of your life that I could have shared and that's making me feel angry, guilty, and empty. Only God knows how much I would love to hear your voice once more. papí, I'm eternally grateful for all you did for me. I wish you were still with me so you could meet your great-grandchildren, so they could have you in their lives the way I had you. I don't know when I will have a chance to come back to see you, and I ask you to forgive me if that takes a long time. Mamí sends her love, but she is still unable to set foot on these grounds. Even now, I believe that her grief due to your loss is too painful, and she misses you dearly. papí..."

Antonio sat in front of Ignacio's grave for more than an hour. He spoke about everything to that tomb as if to let out everything he had inside his traveling soul. He was venting about all that emptiness in his chest. He told his dad that now he knew he was destined to live his life as a foreigner, because the country where he presently lived would always treat him as such, and the country where he was born had already forgotten him. Antonio always thought he was <u>Puerto Rican de pura cepa</u>[36], but lately realized that his homeland had already forgotten him; it seemed he only lived in the memories of all the people who had died in his absence. That feeling was the most difficult to accept because his soul was still part of that place, but he was not. Later, he returned to his mother's house, and he spent the next eleven days visiting his cousin Juan and getting drunk several times. He also visited many places on the Island to recharge his soul before returning to the country where he had his house, but where he had never been able to feel at home. During those eleven days, he again experienced several disappointments, but at night the coquí sang serenades to relieve his pilgrim's pains and in the mornings the birds and roosters lifted him with encouragement.

Finally, the day arrived when Antonio was to return abroad to continue dying in search of a better life. He said goodbye to his mother with a big hug and while she was embracing him, his heart got weary with premonitions and fears of losing her one day. Agustina whispered in her son's ears: *"Never forget where you came from"*. Those words were still ringing in his mind when he sat down on the plane before takeoff. As the plane began to ascend, Antonio continued thinking about those words and thought

---

35. papí: slang for "dad".

36. Puerto Rican de pura cepa: Pure blood Puerto Rican

his mother told him. Although he would never forget the place where he was from, that place had almost forgotten him. For he only lived on the memory of all those people who kept disappearing from his life. So, he went home to wait. To wait for another call that would announce the death of his mother. And with her departure from this world, all the roots connecting him back to his homeland would become in danger of extinction. That damned day when he would realize that his life was filling up with shadows...The shadows of a foreigner's life.

IMPRINTS

T HE LITTLE HOUSE WAS hidden in the middle of a mountain surrounded by woods, in a rural neighborhood of a Puerto Rican town. It was reachable from two routes, an asphalt road connected to the main roads of the town and a dirt path that traversed the mountain in the same way that an artery vein runs through the body. In the eternal summer of the Caribbean sun, the heat and breezes fought to heat up and cool down this humble home that lacked modern conveniences like ceiling fans or air conditioning. Though, in this little house, one could appreciate the different aspects of progress that had occurred throughout the Island's history. The house was a cement structure built with windows that the locals called Miami windows on some of its walls, while other walls had windows that gave the impression of being small doors that remained open all day to welcome the cool breeze. Occasionally, a young boy would visit the house accompanied by his dad. Sometimes the visit was to see the child's padrinos[1] who lived there; sometimes it was to seek relief for their stomach pains. The couple had been the father's friends since childhood and had baptized the boy in the Catholic church as a symbol of their loyalty to him. They would be in the line of succession in the child's upbringing if something happened to his father as was determined by Catholic doctrine. The padrino[2] was a dark-skinned man of medium height, always dressed as

---

1. Padrinos: godparents

2. Padrino: godfather

was customary with a guayabera[3], old dress pants and a short-leaf hat called pava[4]. The madrina[5] was a white-skinned woman of medium height, with gray hair always tied back and sometimes hidden under a pañuelo[6]. She used to wear sleeping robes and was often found wearing rubber flip-flops.

For the child, visits to his padrinos took on an air of curiosity and mystery. He had met them at an early age because his father always took him to visit them regularly. For that reason, he had come to feel comfortable in the little house surrounded by trees. Even so, the little boy always experienced a strange sensation of being in a place that seemed to have been trapped in time. Inexplicably there would be no glimpse of a modern television or radio system. On the walls hung one hand-painted picture of his padrinos in their youth, and nothing else. There was no fancy furniture or ceramic ornaments; there was only a small table in the center of the house in a small room that served as a living room; and in the corner of it, there was a catre[7] on which he had laid more than once during his young life. Still, at six years old the boy had trouble adjusting to the smell inside the house. It wasn't a bad smell, but a smell he couldn't completely identify. At the same time, the smell produced by his padrinos, the smell of them inside their home was so familiar to the little boy; like, the delicious smell of freshly brewed coffee and the smells of the different sweets that he had the pleasure of eating on each visit or after, which he looked forward to. It wasn't those smells that confused him, rather it was the smell of fire and smoke that seemed to confuse his young nose. Another thing he couldn't explain was the reason why the house's yellow walls looked so dull. It appeared as if the house had been painted for the last time a few hundred years before, which even a boy as ignorant as him understood was impossible. And it was those mystical airs and questions that kept the child in a state of amazement with each visit. That and the fact that his godparents made him feel like the most important brat in the whole wide world every time he showed his face in that house.

---

3. Guayabera: lightweight man's shirt with pockets and sometimes tucks or embroidery, worn outside trousers.

4. Pava: straw hat typically associated with Puerto Rican jibaros.

5. Madrina: godmother

6. Pañuelo: handkerchief

7. Catre: cot

The child's madrina, Doña Juana, was the santiguadora[8] of the barrio, a special kind of shaman whose specialty was to alleviate stomach pains with a "doctorate" of experiences in the art of relieving people's pain by doing stomach massages using oils and/or ointments of different kinds. This technique could not be learned at an accredited government university; and there were not that many people who practiced such healings at this time. After all this "unproven" healing method, practiced mostly in remote areas of the country, were being replaced in favor of the science lab and the reliance on taking pills for every ache. However, people around this neighborhood still believed in the effectiveness of the santiguadora and Doña Juana's services were always being sought after.

She also had the religious habit of praying and lighting candles to her favorite saints every time she tended to some sick person who came into her home to see her and lay down on the catre, in the living room, in search of relief from stomach pains. This act of religiosity was very common in the Catholic religion, in which parishioners lighted a candle to a best-loved saint to ask for favors ranging from the economic to the eternal. Even so, the child had no doubt that this wise old woman lit a candle to ask some saint for relief for the many sick persons that she had taken care of over the years. And if the sick went home relieved, in his madrina's eyes, her candle and her prayer had worked a miracle. But what about on other occasions? Did she ever ask for financial relief? or for help with her husband's alcoholism? From what her godson could observe, those prayers had gone without answers. The only thing that he could see was that the walls looked dirty, stained by candle smoke. The cumulative blemishes of smoke on the walls from years of burning candles, as symbols of her faith, had remained wedged into the walls of her humble home. He knew, at a glance, that Doña Juana's personal prayers to God had died trapped in these walls.

For the godson, it was somewhat ironic to realize that his madrina was already about seventy years old at the time when he was just six years old. She served her God with unparalleled and immovable fervor. And in those moments when she worked with her miraculous hands, giving relief to poor sick people, the smoke of the candles continued its relentless path fitting into the walls leaving its dark stains. And from what the child observed, neither the prayers nor the smoke came close to carrying her messages to heaven. She had lit a factory of whole candles to God. And from what the child concluded, the answers to her own needs and desires have not once come to reality. Still, Juana's unshakable faith never

---

8. Santiguadora: shaman who cures stomach pains.

lessened, regardless of the apparent lack of answers. The poverty she and her husband were experiencing was evident even to a six-year-old full of his own. For him, his madrina was the noblest expression of love, patience, and wisdom. And yet the smoke, from her candles to her beloved saints, only served to stain the walls of her poor house. Twenty thousand candles for God, zero answers for her.

As time went by, between prayers and candles, the child became a teenager who still desired to visit and see his madrina, Juana. By then, she was alone because her husband had died when he was about ten years old. There was something about her that calmed his teenage restlessness, something that had stamped his soul as a child and had left its mark, just as the smoke had left its stains on the walls of her house. The youngman did not know the reason for the need to be in that house trapped in time. Even so, with each visit, he still noticed how the fumes of the candles remained stamped on those walls and he could not understand why his madrina's God had not answered her prayers. Apparently, all the saints were very busy, perhaps tending to parishioners of a better economic level. None had bothered to answer her, not even to refund a little money to replenish the matches and candles. And the teenager thought that if that holy woman did not qualify for a divine answer, how would he qualify? Over time the visits became more sporadic and between one visit and another, the years passed and eventually, Doña Juana died like her husband before her. The child's godmother has departed this life after burning a hell in candles to her God to only see the smoke, as well as her life, dissipate in the eternal wait for answers that never came to fruition. Only the candles' fumes remained, stamped on the walls of the santiguera's home, darkening her humble little house that otherwise was always kept clean. Today the child already a man continues to ask himself: *Why does God not answer the prayers of the poor? What must be done so that the smoke from the candles of a poor man's prayers reaches heaven? How is he going to save himself if he has never lit a candle to pray?*

Even today as I'm surrounded by the fog of the sweet memories that I have of my madrina Juana, I remember that the last time I was in her presence, I was only a stranger to her. Madrina's gaze was indifferent to her surroundings, fixed on a wall in her daughter Mena's house, who at that time was her full-time caregiver. I felt as lost as her empty gaze when I came to the realization that my godmother Juana had already died. Her body, already very advanced in age, was about to give up. At that moment, I concluded that I was about to lose one of the most important people in my life. Her body continued to breathe, but her mind had stopped functioning. Time had taken my padrino Goda from her, and Alzheimer's had robbed my madrina of all her memories, memories of her poor and sacrificial life; memories of every candle she lit to her saints, and of course her memories of me. When she asked me repeatedly who I was looking for, it caused me great sadness. Even so, her physical presence continued to provide me with an unparalleled calmness that I hardly experienced in the presence of any other loved one. After a few painful moments, I said goodbye to her, knowing full well that it was possible that I would never see her again. It didn't take long when my madrina Juana's body died a few years after she did when she had forgotten the last memory of her own life.

Today I still carry with me the memories of those visits to my godmother's house with my father, as well as the visits I made of my own free will. I still experience the strange feeling of disappointment in God's apparent neglect for not answering the personal requests that I've always assumed she prayed for, or at least acknowledge the lights and fumes of her candles. And up until now I continue to hold the imprints of her presence in my life because I don't even have a picture of her, and that is all I must remember her by. The mysteries that life holds, that poor woman lit all the candles in the world to her God and I think that without knowing it, the fire of her candles served to illuminate my path in life. Today, I would light a thousand candles to God myself just for the chance to be in the presence of my madrina Juana, one more time. Or at the very least, let me possess a photo of her. So that I could once again contemplate the face of that beautiful woman who only lives in my memory. Because even today the fumes of her candles continue to be engraved in my heart and the fire of her example continues burning brightly in the essence of my soul.

THE GHOST ON THE DIRT PATH

THE SMOKE OF CIGAR filled the air of the place, as did the noises of music produced by the vellonera[1], while Felipe sitting in front of the bar counter watched everything and saw nothing. In one corner the music of the moment consoled some despechado[2] who between songs and rum drowned his sorrows; while, on the other side of it, two men were arguing about the last play at the pool table:

"Compai[3] you didn't call the eight ball, that play doesn't count." -argued the loser.

"I called it before I shot it. -replied the other man visibly upset with the allegation.*"*

"Compai don't cheat me out of my drink; you need to pay up."

"I am not cheating anyone; you just don't want to pay for drinks. You didn't call it."

"Ok. Let's play another round, and the loser pays double this time."

"Deal! Don't start inventing stories when I beat you fair and square."

---

1. Vellonera: jukebox

2. Despechado: heartbroken

3. Compai: slang for compadre.

This inevitable discussion of what is valid or not valid at the pool table was something very common in this place where poor people met to be distracted from the realities of the moment. Near the pool table, were some women dancing alone or with a partner to the beat of a popular song being played on the vellonera. Two of the women commented:

"That song is beautiful." -said one of them, moving to the rhythm of the music.

"Yeah! It's good to help forget your sorrows." -replied the other.

"And is it new?"

"Brand new!!!"

This bar was the perfect destination for the disappointed, the broken-hearted lovers, and the poor in a neighborhood full of poverty. Felipe sat in front of the bar countertop consuming his third or fourth drink of the night. In one hand the shot of rum, and in the other the lit cigar. He was already a fellow in his twenties, already accustomed to the ritual of drowning his poverty in this place that had witnessed so many stories like his. Concentrating on the activities around the bar and while beginning to feel the effects of the alcohol, a voice interrupted his thoughts:

"Another palo[4] compai." - asked the bartender looking at him.

"Yes, <u>uno ma</u>[5] please." -replied Felipe.

"What kind do you want a palo de Candao[6] or a palo of Llave[7] ?"

"Give me one of Llave because I already have the Candao in my body."

"Ok, one palo of Llave coming right up."

Felipe was one of those men who worked in the sugar cane fields, sweetening the world while the bitterness of a poor life was his greatest reality. He earned enough not to starve, but also so little he could not always fill

---

4. Palo: when drinking it means "shot of".

5. Uno ma': slang for "one more".

6. Candao: Local rum, the correct word is candado which translates to "Lock".

7. Llave: Local rum. The name translates to "Key".

his stomach. This Friday he had been paid his salary for the arduous week of work cutting sugar cane under the brutal Caribbean sun, on the Island of Puerto Rico. As it used to happen with a lot of poor people, he already owed most of his salary in the neighborhood's pulperia[8]. However, as a consolation, he would remind himself that at least at this pulperia he could "cojer fiao"[9] once he had settled his accounts. Then, he would have enough money left over to numb his disappointments and sorrows at the bar with music and alcohol. Felipe already had the routine down of mind-numbing his poor economic desperation every payday. On this pay day, after having walked almost five kilometers to his small and humble home from work, he stripped off his dirty clothes and went to the local creek to bathe, right before embarking on the journey to the bar to complete his ritual of drowning his reality. After he had bathed Felipe returned home and dressed in his best Friday attire, shaved his face, and applied some of his favorite cologne Brutt 33 to smell good as any young single man would. Ready for the night he walked to the bar along the dusty dirt path that connected the neighborhood's sectors.

Felipe came to this place for the same reasons as everyone else who was there, to find relief from what caused anguish in his soul. A few hours had passed since his first drink and there had already been talk of how hard the week in the sun had been. How the governor and all the hijos de puta[10] in politics stole everything, and how the church had become unable to connect the poor with God. Sitting at the bar while holding on to the countertop, so as not to fall, he did everything possible to maintain some optimism in the hope of something better. He had inherited his dark-skinned color from his father who was of African descent, as well as his sense of humor; his stature and perseverance were inherited from his mother, who was of medium height and of Spanish descent. Even so, the most obvious inheritance that his parents left him was their endless poverty; from which he suffered since he had a concept of what it meant to be alive.

After many drinks, Felipe felt momentarily relief from his economic and emotional worries. The music of the vellonera together with the people who between games, alcohol, and conversation distracted their lives helped him relax and forget his daily struggles. He also felt a little relief from the

---

8. Pulperia: bodega, corner store

9. Cojer fiao: slang for "buying on the account".

10. Hijos de puta: sons of bitches.

stress of an arduous work week. Around the bar people commented on the goings-on of the Island:

"*¡La piña está agría!*[11] - complained a man standing in from of the bar countertop.

"*It's more sour than green lemons.*"-replied another.

"*But there jay[12] some good moments.*"

"*Yes, but a small amount of those na'ma[13].*"

"*Compadre, another palo of Llave for the poor.*"-yelled one of the men to the bartender.

"*Yes, another palo to enjoy the little things.*"-reaffirmed another man.

So in between drinks, games, conversations and even arguments the afternoon gave way to the night, which in turn gave way to midnight. The time came when the bar was approaching its closing time to give the place and its patrons some time to rest before daylight.

"*We are closing soon.*"- announced the bartender.

"*¡Se acabó lo que se daba!*[14]..."-yelled one of the patrons.

"*Be careful going home and get there safely.*"-advised the bartender.

Felipe was already in an advanced state of drunkenness. He said goodbye to the few people left in the place, staggered out the door, and began his journey back to the solitude of his home. By now, he was so drunk that walking home was like hiking with spaghetti legs, and he could swear to hear his brain sending instructions to his lower limbs so they would move. To reach his destination, he had to cross the roads of the neighborhood in a darkness that was only broken with the moonlight, and this fact worried him a little because his eyes were as drunk as his legs. The dirt trails were like arteries that connected the different sectors of the neighborhood, and these

---

11. ¡La piña está agría!: "The pineapple is sour". local expression to complain about the economic situation.

12. Jay: jibaro word that means "to have".

13. Na'ma: slang for "only that"

14. ¡Se acabó lo que se daba!: local expresion that is like saying it's all over for now.

trails crossed plains as well as hills and mountains in that eternal Caribbean greenery. The established path that would take him home would begin next to the only paved road in and out of the town, and it started at the lower part of the edge of the first hill that Felipe needed to climb to get home. During the trip, the man felt dizzy and staggered down the trail that led him home. At that point, he began to mumble to himself out loud:

"Dammed country, here everyone is fucked except for the politicians. I'm always working, and I'm always screwed. I get up early, walk more than a horse to work like a donkey, and at the week's end I get paid like a child. Fucking politicians always robbing people blind."

Minutes later, he starts another conversation with himself as he walks along the road located precisely in front of the barrio's Catholic church. He makes a sign of reverence to show respect and comments:

"So much for praying and confessing <u>pa'qué</u>[15] , if God doesn't even hear you. Going to church every Sunday to beg God for a change, <u>pa dispue</u>[16] suffer all week long. It doesn't serve me much to pray, it seems that God is always busy paying attention to people that have a lot of money."

When Felipe reached the edge of the first hill, he had to come up with a clever plan to climb this first obstacle without falling backward and desnucarse[17] , as some of his friends and neighbors had done in the past. So, he made the logical decision of turning back time, and as a man that had already reached his late twenties, he decided to learn how to crawl again like a toddler. This was an embarrassing position for Felipe, but at that time of night, nobody was going to see him crawling to the top of the hill. No doubt this was going to take some time, but in the intoxicated state that he was in, it was the best way for him to get home without having some regrettable mishap.

Finally, after what he felt was like an eternity in that embarrassing position, he reached the top of the hill. Now he had the difficult task of traveling downhill to the next plane on the dirt trail that would connect him with the next path that would lead him home. This time Felipe decided to use his next strategy; he would go down the hill dragging his butt on the floor doing squats. That way he would avoid falling and fracturing any bones.

---

15. Pa'qué: slang for "for what"

16. Pa'dispue: slang for "to later on"

17. Desnucarse: to break his neck.

Dragging his ass along the road and from squat to squat he undertook the embarrassing journey to the bottom of the hill. Again, he thought about the humiliation of his position, but his logic was firm: *"If I'm on the floor I can't fall."* The moonlight illuminated the way and, already with his pants full of dust, Felipe had reached the middle of the downhill when in the distance he observed a translucent white figure, one that he immediately identified as an apparition or better known to him as a ghost. This vision made him climb back to the top of the hill in a crawling position. At that moment fear overcame logic, and he tried to run upwards on his spaghetti legs only to fall backwards, which a few minutes before he had tried to avoid at all costs. He got up and again tried to run upwards, but this time he felt forward. Once again, he started to crawl quickly until he had reached the top of the hill.

Already at the top of the hill, his heart continued beating fast inside his chest. Though, the fear seemed to have taken his drunkenness away, and he began to review the events in which ghosts of different shapes and sexes had appeared to many inhabitants of the place. The headless woman who had asked his compadre for his underpants to wash them in the creek; the crying woman who cried out in pain for the loss of a great love; and the ghost who had visited his own body to mourn his own death and other stories. The more he thought about this, the more afraid he felt. So, he began to reassess the decisions that had led him to this peculiar situation. Felipe started with the most obvious of conclusions, there was no ghost in the way, it was that he was drunk and was imagining things.

"Shit, it seems like se me pasó la mano[18] *with El candao and La Llave."* - he said to himself.

A short time later, he got up from the ground where he was still sitting, terrified of the unknown apparition. Looking up towards the path and not seeing anything out of the ordinary, he decided to climb back down the hill, and get home. Once more, Felipe had reached the middle of the descent when he managed to notice the white figure moving from side to side on his path home. In between multiple falls and stumbles, he could feel his heart pounding as he reached the top of the hill, once again.

There on the hill, he reflected looking for reasons why a ghost was haunting him. First, he analyzed how he behaved with people, especially his family, his friends, and his neighbors. He thought about the times when he failed to contribute to his mother's well-being. He deduced from his behavior

---

18. Se me pasó la mano: Like saying "I went overboard".

that his friends were only bar friends with whom he drank and nothing else. Regarding his neighbors, well fuck the neighbors, because they gossip about everything but never contribute anything.

"What's the reason for this ghost?" -he asked himself repeatedly.

"Why now? If I haven't done <u>na'malo</u>[19]. I treat my vieja[20] well, and I help people whenever I can. Why me?"

Still sitting at the top of the hill with a ghost waiting for him on the road ahead and with no options on how to get rid of it, Felipe began to take a mental journey about the truths of his existence. This turning point in his life gave way to having an honest conversation with himself:

"Maybe I deserve this for not helping my vieja. She is alone all week since papí[21] died and my siblings left. She washes my dirty clothes in the quebra[22] and cooks for me all week. And what do I do, na[23]. Every time I get money; I drink it all and I don't help her. I must get my drinking under control, so I can take care of my vieja."

A few minutes passed before Felipe once again tried to continue his arduous trip home; yet hesitated when he saw the ghost still waiting for him up ahead. Maybe it was there to solve some outstanding problem he possibly had with some deceased friend or enemy. So, he stayed at the top of the hill and continued analyzing his precarious situation:

"Could it be because I don't help other people? After all, I'm always in a bad mood. When was the last time I helped someone? I don't remember. <u>Pa' decil la veldad</u>[24] I have never helped anyone. A bottle of rum's my only friend. I must stop drinking once and for all."

---

19. Na'malo: slang for "nothing bad"

20. Vieja: old woman used as a term of endearment.

21. papí: slang for "dad".

22. Quebra: slang for "creek".

23. Na': slang for "nothing".

24. Pa decil la veldad: slang for "to tell the thruth"

The moon was beginning its ritual descent, while Felipe was still struggling to find a feasible solution to his ghost problem. Two hours passed since he laid eyes on the specter. Apparently, the ghost would wait for him until he decided to get there and hold the anticipated conversation Felipe was trying to avoid for hours. This is how he resolved to make an emergency call to the heavens, hoping that this time God would not place him on hold for too long, as it always happened all his life.

"My God help me pol favol[25], I'm not a bad person. If you help me tonight, I promise that I will take care of my vieja and I will try to be helpful to others, de ahora en adelante[26]. Pol favol help me, and I will go to church to ressal[27]. God help me please. If you help me, I promise you that I will stop drinking, I will not touch a palo of rum anymore."

When he spoke these words Felipe felt great emptiness in his heart, because for him getting drunk was his only relief from the reality of the harshness of his life. He had no memory of a time in his life when he wasn't drinking constantly. Felipe was an alcoholic by inheritance as he had inherited this habit from his father, Don Manuel. He knew no other way to distract himself from his apparent discontent with life. He used alcoholic drinks and smoked tobacco to cloud his mind forgetting the fact that he was illiterate, a loner, and not a very religious person. For that last reason, Felipe never envisioned himself asking for miracles. Miracles, he always thought, were predestined for the rich and powerful. He was just another jodío[28] in the world, an alcoholic whose only purpose in life was to work as a donkey all week to then spend his free time drunk trying to forget his own misery. Nevertheless, a ghost was waiting for him on the trail, and in situations like these it was better to promise God a change than to have to sell his unworthy soul to the devil. Who knew what the ghost wanted? So, Felipe decided it was better to take his chances with God.

Three hours went by since Felipe had laid eyes on the specter. Exhausted with the weight of a week's work, with alcohol running through his bloodstream, with dusty pants, and with urine that at some point had escaped from his nervous body just like his courage escaped him when he first spotted the white translucent figure, Felipe decided to gamble with

---

25. Pol favol: slang for "please"

26. de ahora en adelante: moving forward

27. Ressal: slang for "praying".

28. Jodío: fucked.

his luck. Because up to this point nothing else had worked. So again, he attempted his descent down the hill, determined to pay for whatever sin he had committed. More importantly, he had already settled his accounts with God and was armed with a spiritual courage that no ghost could overcome. Now he was a newborn Christian, although it was by necessity only.

As Felipe got closer to the inevitable encounter with the apparition, his fear was evident. His heart jumped up terrified inside his chest. He decided that it was better to close his eyes just in case the ghost was scarier than he had imagined. He continued walking until he reached the approximate location where the ghost would be; however, overcome by curiosity, he opened his eyes. When he was finally able to look at the ghost face to face, what a surprise! Felipe felt confusion, anger, and shame; and he knew right there and then that these eventful feelings would be repressed forever in his heart. In the spot where the ghost was waiting for him, he instead saw a yagrumo[29] bush that the breezes blowing up over the hill and down into the valley, moving from side to side.

In an act of rage, he grabbed the bush and uprooted it; at the same time cursing at it for wasting his time and causing him to anguish all night long imagining it was a ghost. After demolishing the yagrumo bush into a thousand pieces, Felipe sat down on the road drained, dirty, and urinated. He threw himself backward and began to laugh like a madman. The relief he felt was evident amidst his joy and his crazy laughter, he analyzed everything he had thought about that night. After a few minutes, he rose from the ground while looking at the top of the hill and the side of the trail where the yagrumo bush had been planted a few moments before. Then he turned his gaze to the path ahead and continued towards his home. When he got there, he entered his chamber, took off his clothes full of dust and urine and sat semi-naked on the edge of his catre[30] from where the <u>almanaque de hoja</u>[31] that was hanging on the wall, caught his eye.

Felipe got up to tear a leaf off the calendar to represent a new time for milestones, and a new day to rest and forget the many promises that he made that night while urinating on himself in fear. He flipped through the leaves of the calendar and hastily came up with the best idea of the night,

---

29. Yagrumo: Yagrumo: species of trees that grow in P.R. Its leaves appear to shine when humid and under the moonlight.

30. Catre: cot

31. almanaque de hoja: daily flip calendar

to mark off a special day on the calendar. Felipe marked off the best day to forget what needed to be forgotten, and his answer was awaiting him in a stool at the barrio's bar the very next Friday.

UNDER THE FLAMBOYÁN

A T DAWN, THE MORNING'S silence was shattered by a rooster pro-
claiming "good morning" with his cu, cu, ru, cu, cu. His crowing
marked the beginning of a new day by awakening the Puerto Rican neighborhood from its slumber, while the coquí took its rest after serenading
the mountains and hills with its nightly habit of repeating its name all
night long. Then the houses gradually came to life, candles, quimques[1],
and light bulbs flickered on, illuminating the residents' paths. The enticing
aroma of coffee soon wafted through the air, bringing a pleasant scent
around the mountains where the place was located. Doors swung open one
by one, as the neighborhood's men set off for work. Their synchronized
routine created a symphony of opening and closing doors, for most of
them were employed by the same company. However, amidst the bustling
activity, there was one door that remained closed. Although the light from
the quimqué was visibly flickering, there was no trace of coffee aroma or
anyone inside the house preparing to go to work.

Inside the house, Pablo sat on the edge of a worn-out armchair, his gaze
fixed upon the floor, lost in thought. Troubled and despondent, he pondered over the course of his day. In the only bedroom of the house, his
children slept, huddled together on an improvised bunk bed made of
wood. He rose from his seat with great effort to check the lacena[2] and
take stock of the food that remained inside it. There was a can of coffee
that was almost empty, a can of sardines, a jar of salt, a few cans of tomato

---

1. Quimques: oil lamps

2. Lacena: pantry

sauce, and a small amount of sugar in an improvised container. Today, he wouldn't brew coffee until his children woke up, ensuring there was enough for everyone. After assessing the poverty-stricken inventory, he opened the door and made his way to the letrina[3] to relieve himself and empty the punchera[4]. On his return, he checked the hens' nests, hoping they had left some eggs for breakfast to alleviate the hunger of his children, who, like him, had been left orphaned when their mother fled from their home running from their poverty and leaving them all behind.

Pablo who was already in his forties, had been unemployed since the previous year when a near-fatal accident had almost killed him while working for the town's most profitable construction company on the Island. He had fallen from a second story building while he was standing on a scaffold. Pablo had been enpañetando[5] a wall when the scaffold beneath him shifted, causing him to plummet to the pavement below, striking his head and losing consciousness. After being hospitalized and treated for several days, he was sent home to embark on a long and slow recovery. The doctor had prescribed rest, but he needed money to sustain himself and his family. After a few weeks of inactivity, he embarked on the arduous journey of rehabilitation, as his injured back made it exceedingly difficult to perform the tasks required by his job before the accident. Months passed, and he returned to his workplace, ready to work as he had done for over two decades. However, his body was no longer the same. Initially, his employers had shown sympathy for the challenges he faced while trying to fulfill his duties. Yet, as time passed by, their understanding transformed into disappointment, almost bordering on hostility towards their employee, who had dedicated the best years of his life to the company. One day, Pablo arrived at work early, as he usually did, and the foreman immediately approached him.

"Amigo[6], can we talk for a moment?" -the foreman asked.

"Of course, jefe[7]." -Pablo replied.

"Please, come to my office in a few minutes."

---

3. Letrina: outhouse

4. Punchera: chamber pot

5. Enpañetando: wall paneling.

6. Amigo: friend

7. Jefe: boss

"There is something wrong, jefe?"

"Don't worry about it, we'll discuss it in private in my office."

A short while later, Pablo stood outside the foreman's office, knocking on the door to seek permission to enter.

"Come in!" -a voice responded from within.

"Good morning, <u>puedo pasar</u>[8] ?" -asked Pablo timidly.

"Come in and have a seat." -instructed the foreman as Pablo entered.

"Is there something wrong?" -he asked again.

"Well, my amigo, we need to talk." -replied the foreman with a somber look on his face.

"What's the matter jefe? Did I do something wrong?"

"Amigo, you've been with us for over twenty years, and we genuinely appreciate your dedication. However, since your injury, your productivity has declined, and we can no longer keep you employed."

"<u>¿Me están botando?</u>[9] After all these years of working here, you're just throwing me out? <u>Pol favol!</u>[10] Jefe, I have children to support, and I'm the only breadwinner."

"Believe me Pablo, it breaks our hearts to make this decision, but at the end of the day, this is a business, and we need able-bodied workers to fulfill the tasks at hand. You know how it is."

"But you know I'm a responsible and hardworking man. I'll do whatever you ask, just don't fire me. Pol favol do me this favol[11] ."

"Yes, I know you've always been willing to go the extra mile, but trust me when I tell you that this decision is not up to me."

---

8. puedo pasar: Can I come in?

9. ¿Me están botando?: are you firing me?

10. Pol favol!: slang for "please".

11. Favol: Slang for "favor".

"Then whose decision it is, the owner? Can I talk to the owner?"

"I'm afraid that wouldn't be prudent. Those people don't care about anything but money."

"Please, you're leaving me desempleao[12], and I can't afford that. Remember that I got injured while working for you. Have some consideration, please. My children depend on me to provide for them."

"I understand, Amigo. Believe me, I do. But this decision is final, and I can't change it. I ask you to take it easy. Go home, calm down, something will come up eventually. Please forgive me, it's not what I wanted to do."

"I understand, jefe, I understand. It's just that I'll be in a tough spot with my kids and no job."

The reality was that the foreman felt terrible about the decision, but he himself was just another employee. He had spent days pleading with the owners to find some other position for their employee, as he was one of the most loyal, they had. But it didn't matter how much he pleaded for the man with a broken body, it didn't make a difference. The employer had calculated the costs, and money outweighed the loyalty the man had shown them over the years. Unfortunately, this was the reality for many employees. There were no safeguards or protections in place to shield them from the risks and abuse they faced while enriching their employers who controlled local politicians and municipalities.

It had been over a year since the day when Pablo was let go from his job. Today, while the other men in the neighborhood were working to support their families, he was burdened with constant worries about providing the bare necessities for his children. A roof over their heads and their daily sustenance. He had applied for numerous jobs, but he was rejected everywhere due to his less-than-optimal health. No one wanted to hire someone with his physical limitations. Resigned to the fact that he may never work again, he had resorted to taking sporadic odd jobs in the neighborhood. However, in a place where most people were as impoverished as he was, such opportunities were scarce and inconsistent. Nevertheless, a few of his neighbors occasionally offered him temporary work like cutting grass, painting or cleaning yards which allowed him to earn some money without having to ask for any handouts or help.

---

12. Desempleao: slang for "unemployed".

After making a laborious trip to the latrine to empty the punchera, Pablo made his way to a bucket of water to wash his hands and face. Then he entered his humble home and placed a pot on the stove to boil some eggs laid by the hens the previous night, while they were enjoying the serenade of coquíes. After cooking hard boiled eggs in boiling water and brewing a pot of coffee for breakfast, he served his children a meager meal that would help them have something in their stomachs, so they wouldn't feel too hungry. Shortly after, he sat on a makeshift wooden bench under a vibrant flamboyán[13] tree, which stood out with its red color amidst the greenery of the mountainous neighborhood.

Sitting beneath the tree, Pablo considered his next steps. First, he planned to check the nearby pana[14] tree to see if any fruits were ripe for eating. Next, carrying his machete and pickaxe, he would then venture into the mountains to search for ñames [15], if the panas were not ready. Last, either option, the panas or the ñames would be mixed with the last can of sardines to provide a meal for his children. This had become his daily life since his unfortunate accident. For him, everything seemed to move slowly or backward since that fateful incident. After a few minutes of contemplation, he settled off into the mountains accompanied by his eldest son, Octavio, to search for their sustenance of the day. Due to his limited mobility, the search would take them hours. Carrying a machete, pickaxe, sack, and a small battery-powered radio for music and news updates, they embarked on their journey.

First, they arrived at the pana tree only to find that the fruits were not yet ripe. Then they continued deeper into the mountain, hoping to find ñame bejucos[16] that marked the spot where they had to dig up the root vegetable. However, after twenty minutes of searching, they found none in sight. They ventured further inside the forest and after over an hour, they discovered the buried treasure. Pablo and his son began the laborious task of digging up the day's food. To create space for their work, he cleared the surrounding bushes, instructing his son to do the same.

"You need to clear all the bejucos around." -Pablo told his son Octavio.

---

13. Flamboyán: a tree with red flowers that bears no fruit.

14. Pana: breadfruit.

15. ñames : yams roots.

16. Bejucos: vines.

"Why? -asked his son with an annoyed look."

"So that when you're using the pickaxe, you won't hit the bejucos and injure yourself with it."

"But that's more work." -complained Octavio.

"It's more work, but we must do it if we want to eat today."

"Is there nothing else to eat today?"

"We have a can of sardines and that's it."

"And what about tomorrow?"

"Let's focus on today's meal first, and we'll figure it out for tomorrow later. Cut the bejucos.

-Okay, papí[17]."

While the boy cleared the bejucos around the ñame root, Pablo turned on the radio to keep himself entertained during the excavation. A cheerful song played, momentarily distracting him from the weight of his thoughts. After two uninterrupted songs, the announcer shared the day's news, filled with lies and deception of the political class. They spoke of progress and societal advancements, painting a rosy picture of a prosperous world that Pablo had never witnessed, living in his bleak reality.

"These malditos[18] politicos[19] feast on their own lies." -he muttered in frustration.

The radio interrupted the news once again, this time to announce the high jackpot of the lottery, encouraging people to try their luck. Upon hearing this, Pablo, in his desperation, searched his pockets and found three dollars. He began calculating what provisions were left in the lacena to see how much he could spare to spend on lottery tickets. For a moment, he allowed himself to dream about the odds of winning the lottery and the possibilities of a prize such as a large sum of money, and what this money could provide. Imagining the things he could buy and give to his

---

17. Papí: slang for "dad".

18. Malditos: dammed

19. Politicos: politicians

children, a better home, food, a good education, and relief from their current hardships. Then his son's voice brought him back to reality:

"Papí, I've finished trimming the bejucos around the ñame." -Octavio announced.

"Alright, now we need to dig a hole to get the ñame." -replied Pablo.

"Okay, give me the pickaxe so I can start."

"Here it is but be careful not to break the ñame underground."

"Don't worry, papí. I've dug up ñames before."

"And you always complain about the preparation work before you dig."

"I know. It's because I don't really like ñames that much."

"I know mijo [20] *but se hace lo que se pue* [21] *."*

Octavio began digging a hole a few inches away from the ñame's bejuco. Little by little, a shallow hole began to take shape. Pablo asked his son to check if the root of the ñame that was now exposed beyond the hole's depth, was big enough. After a few moments, he knelt in front of the hole and started digging the earth with both hands. In a matter of minutes, the size of the ñame became visible, but they realized it wasn't enough to feed the whole family. Determined to find more ñames, they continued their search in the mountains, hoping to stave off hunger for at least one more day. By two o'clock in the afternoon, carrying half a sack of ñames, father and son returned home. The other children would help peel the root vegetables while Pablo prepared the wood for the fogón. [22] They settled to cook the meal on the fogón to save propane gas, which was running low. Afterward, the family would enjoy the ñames with a mixture of sardines. Then all the children took off to play around the neighborhood while waiting for the food to be ready.

Once again, Pablo sat beneath the fiery red flamboyán tree, lost in thought, planning his next food-gathering expedition for his children. The nearby drum radio played contemporary music, and the local news highlighted

---

20. Mijo: slang for 'my son".

21. se hace lo que se pue: jibaro way of saying "we do what we can".

22. Fogón: woodstove.

the lives of small birds. The lottery commercial echoed through the air, promising luck, and riches to anyone who bought a ticket. He reached into his pockets, still holding three dollars, and calculated once more if he could afford to buy a lottery ticket and avoid going hungry at the same time. Pablo dreamed of the possibility that this could be his lucky day, the day he could finally escape the desperate situation that had haunted him for over a year. This time it was his daughter, Marta, who brought him back to the present:

"Papí, I think the ñames are ready." -said Marta.

"Okay, let me check." -he replied, walking over to the fogón to test the softness of the ñame with a knife.

"Are they ready?" -Marta asked again.

"Yes, mija, they are ready. Call the others to eat while I prepare the mextura[23]."

"Alright, Papí."

Pablo entered the kitchen, opened the lacena and surveyed its contents. He found a can of sardines and took stock of what remained, a little bit of coffee grounds, a little bit of sugar, and mostly empty space. He leaned against the lacena's door and let out a sigh of disappointment and despair. With his three dollars, he would have to visit the pulperia[24] and find creative ways to stretch his money, so he had enough left over to buy something for the next morning. After preparing the sardines, he stepped out to serve a plate of ñames with a little bit of sardines to each of his children, urging them to eat before heading to the nearby quebrada[25] for a bath, a makeshift solution for those who couldn't afford proper showers facilities in their homes. Afterwards, Pablo went by himself to the pulperia to purchase provisions for the next day.

It was customary that every day after dinner, he would send his children to bathe while he did other things. On this day, he headed to the pulperia with the little money he had. True to form, he once again spent a portion of it on lottery tickets; then, stopped by the church on his way home to seek divine blessings for his hopeful purchase. Back at home, he replenished

---

23. Mextura: mixture or the mix refers to a side dish to accompany the main food.

24. Pulperia: bodega, corner store.

25. Quebrada: creek

the meager supplies in the lacena, finding a slightly improved situation compared to two days ago, offering a brief respite from the worries of providing for his children. Tomorrow, he hoped, the lottery might free them from their desperate circumstances.

It had all happened very quickly, as at the precise moment when the radio aired the lottery commercial again, his desperation had reached its peak when he stepped into the pulperia, with only three dollars that remained from his last sporadic job he had performed for a neighbor. Pablo knew that finding employment with his injured body was a bleak prospect, which had been the case for a while now. Then he began searching for the most affordable provisions he could purchase with his meager funds. As he selected items worth nearly three dollars, despair clouded his thoughts and in a moment of weak resolve, he returned some items to their original shelves and saved enough to buy a lottery ticket.

On his way home, he found himself standing in front of the town's Catholic church, seeking solace and divine intervention. With a heartfelt plea, he implored God for a favor, not asking for wealth but simply for his children to be spared from hunger. Praying for a stroke of luck, his heart brimmed with hope, believing that his spontaneous prayer would receive a positive response from God.

As the sun began its descent, he had arranged his modest purchases in the lacena and returned to his spot beneath the flamboyán tree. This time, a glimmer of hope enveloped him, even though the lottery drawing was still two days away. Fueled by the belief that his ticket had been blessed and that God would not forsake him in this cruel moment, he clung to the last little bit of hope within his heart that things were about to change for his family.

The night embraced him as he sat beneath the tree, his spirit uplifted by the melodies that filled the air. Each mention of the possibility of luck in the lottery stirred excitement within him. Weary from the day's worries and drained by its demands, Pablo sought solace in the fresh waters of the nearby quebrada, bathing to refresh his tired soul. Upon returning home, he settled into his bed, ready to surrender to sleep's embrace hoping to stop his worries for at least five or six hours.

The next day began once more with the crowing of the rooster and the neighborhood stirring from its slumber. Once again, the warm glow of house lights and the enticing aroma of freshly brewed coffee filled the air. One by one, men set off to work, while Pablo sat in his worn-out armchair, contemplating the day ahead and how he would provide food for his children.

He opened the lacena, taking stock of its meager contents once more. Then he ventured to the hen nests, hoping that some eggs were laid by his hens the previous night and they would help him provide a modest breakfast for his kids. Once again, he found himself boiling eggs on the stove, a meager offering to quell the hunger of his little ones. Holding breakfast in his hands, he made his way to his favorite bench beneath the flamboyán tree.

Sitting there, pondering the day and how he could ensure his children's nourishment, the man ruminated on the injustice of his predicament. He was a diligent worker who had been rendered unable to toil any longer by a freak accident. He despised the notion of relying on charity and felt burdened when neighbors occasionally helped. Pablos's father, Don Tito, had instilled in him the value of earning a living through hard work, making it difficult for him to ask for assistance without feeling worthless. Despite the pain due to his ailments resulting from a broken back, he decided to go fishing in the town's river nearby, in search of the tilapia fish that swam within. This time, he brought along two of his children for company and help.

Arriving at the river, they cast their fishing lines with hope in their hearts, longing for a bountiful catch to sustain them for the day. The fishing proved fruitful, and after a few hours, they had enough to satiate their hunger. Still, Pablo and his sons continued to fish, not willing to squander the opportunity. It was then that one of his children asked:

"Papí, don't we have enough already?" -Raúl asked.

"Yes, we have enough, but we can sell a few in the neighborhood." -replied Pablo.

"And how much are we going to sell them for?"

"For whatever we can, so we can get <u>un poco the chavos</u>[26] ."

"Papí remember that we can't carry much, and you can't carry much either, because the heavy load is going to create more strain on your back." -Octavio reminded him while Raúl looked on.

"I know, but we must do something."

While Pablo and his children embarked on their fishing adventure, the soothing melodies and informative broadcasts emanating from their

---

26. Un poco de chavos: slang for " a little bit of money".

portable radio accompanied them. Amidst the music and news, the persistent lottery commercial continued its relentless pursuit of victims, enticing every impoverished listener with dreams of a better life. Just as before, the man found himself drifting into daydreams, contemplating the possibilities of becoming the fortunate winner. The distant prospect, coupled with his desperate prayer to God, had sparked a flicker of hope within the destitute man. The amalgamation of despair and faith enveloped him, momentarily lifting the weight of his poverty and presenting him with fleeting visions of what could be. However, one of his sons gently nudged him back to the present, grounding him once again in their reality:

"Papí, don't you think we already have enough to eat and sell?" -Raúl said.

"I think so, we are going to pick up the threads, clean the fish and leave early to sell some and to eat. Then we will all go down to the quebra to bathe." -Pablo replied.

After spending a few minutes cleaning the fish, they had caught, the trio made their way back home. Pablo instructed his children to go around the neighborhood, offering the freshly caught fish to the neighbors who had supported them before. Meanwhile, he set about cooking the fish they would enjoy for their afternoon meal. Together with his daughter Marta, he prepared a flavorful marinade, adding a sprinkle of salt for taste. The boys returned after having sold the fish and earning around six dollars in profit. Grateful for their assistance, Pablo expressed his appreciation, and the children beamed with joy, glad to contribute to the well-being of their home.

Following dinner, he sent his children off to bathe as dictated by their daily routine. Meanwhile, he made his way to the pulperia with the money he had earned from the sale. Still, in desperation mode he allocated a portion of his funds to purchase lottery tickets, hoping for a stroke of luck. On his way back home, he paused in front of the church again, seeking divine blessings for the tickets he held tightly. Arriving home, he replenished the meager contents of the lacena. Although there wasn't much, it was more than what they had three days ago, providing momentary relief from the worry of how he would feed his children the next day. After all, tomorrow marked the day when the lottery could potentially free them from their pressing need.

As was his custom since his wife had abandoned him and left their children behind, he sought solace under the shelter of the leafy flamboyán tree near his house. The sight of the reddish fallen flowers surrounding him brought a small sense of calm to his otherwise turbulent existence. Nighttime had arrived when a gentle rain began to fall between his moments of tranquility and his contemplative thoughts. Initially, the drizzle was light and failed to dampen the entire area, but soon it intensified, turning into hard rainfall. Just like that Pablo found answers to his concerns about their next day's meal. He entered his house, grabbed a quimque and an empty sack, and asked one of his children to prepare to venture out into the downpour.

"Papí, where are we going in this heavy rain?" -José asked confused.

"To catch buruquenas[27] in the quebra." -Pablo replied.

"To which area are we going?"

"To the quebra[28] by compai[29] Aurelio's place."

Drenched by the pouring rain, they embarked on their journey, filled with hope for the opportunity to capture buruquenas at that location. Their plan involved traversing the quebrada, checking beneath any palm trees they encountered, as it was widely known that buruquenas emerged to feast on the seeds of palm trees that fell during rainy days. Before reaching their destination, Pablo reminded his son of his responsibilities for the excursion:

"Remember, if you spot one, don't startle it by getting too close, or it'll scuttle away." -Pablo instructed his son.

"I know, Papí." -replied the boy.

"Remember not to keep the light pointed at them for long or they will get scared and scatter away."

"Ok, Papí."

"First, I'll search for them in the usual cuevas[30], and as we walk, we'll stop near the palm trees to search beneath them."

"Hopefully, we'll catch enough to sell a few."

---

27. Buruquenas: black river crabs

28. Quebra: slang for "creek".

29. Compai: slang for "compadre".

30. Cuevas: caves

"¡Que Dios te oiga mijo![31] *"*

After walking for a couple of minutes on the main road, they took a dirt trail to their destination. They reached the road leading to the place, lighting the quimque before venturing into the immense darkness of the quebrada, shrouded in the undergrowth. Their first task was to investigate the small cuevas near the water, where the buruquenas were known to seek refuge. The search began slowly, and in the initial minutes, they found no signs of their elusive prey. However, as they stumbled upon the first palm tree along the route, they discovered two of them. As they continued along the treacherous path, father and son engaged in sporadic conversations about various matters, including the boy's school and other topics. The expedition lasted around four hours, and by the end of the nocturnal hunting, they had managed to secure about ten buruquenas. It wasn't a significant haul for selling purposes, but mixed in yellow rice, it would stave off hunger for another day.

As a new day emerged, dampened by the previous night's rainfall, Friday had arrived. The man followed his usual morning routine, disposing of the accumulated night's urine, tending to the chickens, and collecting their promising eggs. With coffee brewed, he served his children a modest meal of bread and eggs. Then, he retreated to his customary spot beneath the flamboyán tree.

Noticing an abundance of red flowers strewn across the ground, remnants of the heavy rainfall, Pablo observed the aftermath of nature's downpour. Today, there were no plans to search for hidden treasures of buried food, nor to venture out for fishing. Instead, he already had ten buruquenas gathered in a bucket of water, ready to be cooked with rice. The day's plan revolved around waiting for a miraculous stroke of luck while engaging in various tasks to kill time until the lottery results were announced. The man clung to his faith, believing that his prayers had been heard and that the outcome of the raffle would be in his favor.

As the afternoon approached, signaling the nearing of his destiny, Pablo switched on the radio. Amid the blend of music and commercials, he anxiously awaited the lottery draw results. Only five numbers away, and tomorrow he wouldn't have to endure the empty lacena or resort to pilfering eggs from hens or venturing into the wilderness to scrounge for food. This was the moment of truth when the man's yearning to provide for his children led him to invest some of his meager funds in the hope that a

---

31. ¡Que Dios the oiga mijo!: may God hear you my son.

numerical dream would become a happy reality. After a few minutes, the radio announced the winning numbers. Afterward, Pablo's gaze fell into despair, the stark reality of emptiness sinking in. The jackpot would not be his, and tomorrow he would once again be thrust into the perpetual struggle for survival.

As he had done countless times before, the disheartened man let the lottery tickets slip from his grasp, surrendering to the brokenness of his existence. He was willing to work, yet opportunities eluded him. He was willing to implore divine mercy, but it proved fruitless. He was willing to try anything except begging for help. Beneath the flamboyán tree, he sat, much like other impoverished souls worldwide who played the lottery. Praying, and spending money they didn't possess on tickets that, like the flamboyán flowers, offered a momentary escape into a different hue, a temporary respite from their harsh reality. Yet, it was all a mirage, for the flamboyán flowers held the same chance of bearing fruit as a destitute person did of winning the lottery. And beneath that flamboyán tree, Pablo would spend the rest of his life weaving dreams of wealth and economic stability to forever be consumed by the unattainable allure of impossible riches, while spending his days crushed by the lottery of an eternal poverty.

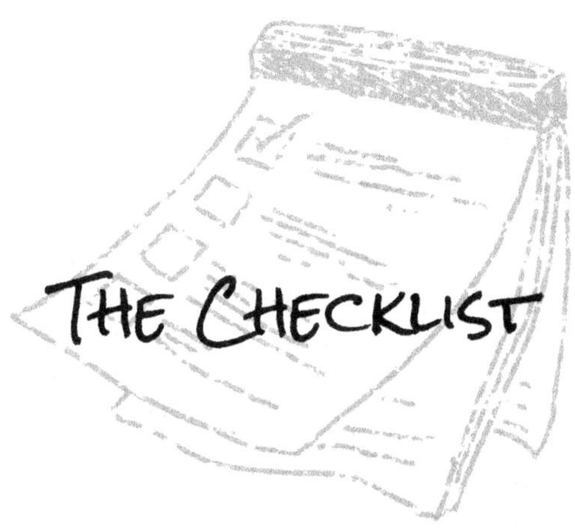

THE CHECKLIST

THE COQUÍ[1] SERENADED THE morning with its melodious tunes, accompanied by the pitirres[2], creating an atmosphere of what appeared to be a flawless day. As Jorge awakened, he welcomed a sliver of sunlight into his room and rose from his bed. Anticipation filled his chest, for this was the day he had meticulously planned for and eagerly awaited. He walked to a glass window to peek outside, to verify that the day would be as close to perfect as he had hoped for. In what felt like an instant, he found himself immersed in a bath of warm water, set precisely to his liking. He dressed appropriately, deliberately going over the day's itinerary in his mind as if he had pondered it for an eternity. Nothing and no one would hinder the unfolding of this day according to his vision. Jorge stepped into his vehicle, igniting the engine with a sense of purpose. He made a single call, the only one he would initiate or answer on this momentous day. Across the telephone line, a voice affirmed his request, setting the plan into motion. It was time to embark on his journey from the bustling city of San Juan to a Puerto Rican barrio[3], nestled amidst fields.

The journey ahead encompassed approximately forty-five minutes of travel, navigating through roads that commenced within an exclusive residential area of San Juan. It would then traverse the expressway, leading towards the familiar paths of the barrio where he spent his formative years. On

---

1. coquí: species of frog that can only survive in Puerto Rico

2. Pitirre: El Pitirre (Tyrannus dominicensis) one of the best-known birds in Puerto Rico

3. Barrio: a neighborhood

this auspicious day, he would pick up his father, Don Rodulfo. This was a meaningful family occasion he had meticulously planned for what seemed like an eternity.

As he embarked on this trip along roads that would guide him back to his childhood barrio, the green landscapes served as a picturesque backdrop. Jorge mentally reviewed every detail he had planned for, creating a mental checklist that he was determined to complete on this important day. By the end of it, each item on the list was to be marked with a checkmark of completion, thus leaving no question unanswered. And with divine intervention, he hoped to offer his own insights and resolve the inner turmoil that plagued his soul. This visit was a quest to reconnect with a part of himself that he had left behind in that humble barrio. As he reached the threshold of the house that had witnessed his upbringing, he paused to reflect upon his journey to success from the depths of poverty. This very place had witnessed his first tentative steps and inevitable stumbles in this world. Contemplating the transformation from a disadvantaged resident of this barrio to someone who had achieved more in life, he pondered the possibilities that unfolded before him on this specific date.

With these profound thoughts swirling in his mind, Jorge entered the realm of his memories. Inside the living room, he found his father, Don Rodulfo, still surrounded by the constant reminders of his everlasting poverty, sitting on the same old sofa where he had left him many years ago, after the death of his mother Adelaida. Both men, almost strangers to one another, had agreed upon a suitable attire for this special occasion. He approached his father and enveloped him in a tight embrace, longing for a connection that would endure beyond the confines of time. In return, his father embraced him with equal intensity, his gaze devoid of reproach, conveying only deep affection and love for his estranged son. Right there amidst the humble surroundings of his father's abode, Jorge began to address the questions on his preconceived list. Each interaction, every shared moment, became an opportunity to place checkmarks of completion beside the unresolved questions, gradually finding solace in the reunification of their souls.

From the house, the two men boarded the first-born son's vehicle heading for the second step on the itinerary. In the blink of an eye, the two found themselves sitting in a fonda[4] known to both and where the search for answers would officially begin. The fonda, typical of an era virtually nonexistent presently in Puerto Rico, had the usual countertop with red

---

4. Fonda: home or small establishment that serves cooked meals.

spinning bar stools. More than once the father had corrected his son, for pretending to use the stools as a spinning wheel, found in an amusement park. The owner of the place, for some mystical or inexplicable reason, still had the same physical appearance he had during Jorge's childhood. The walls of the fonda appeared dirty with time. They were not dirty for lack of hygiene; these walls simply seemed full of stains left by the passing of time and years of service assisting all its customers, who crossed its doors in search of relief from their hunger. Their cravings were satisfied with a cup of coffee or a <u>Desayuno Criollo</u>[5]; or home-made juice from the country made with acerolas[6], or parchas[7], or tamarindo[8] to accompany a <u>Mixta Criolla</u>[9] . In that fonda there was everything for everyone in a town that belonged to nobody.

At a cozy but very old table tucked away in a quiet corner, sat Jorge and Don Rodulfo, their presence gracing the occasion while the fonda appeared strangely deserted. Savoring the flavor and smell of their cups of steaming coffee and relishing a plate of delectable Desayuno Criollo, they embarked on a conversation that meandered through the labyrinth of time, in pursuit of answers long yearned. Jorge initiated the dialogue, delving into inquiries about his father's past. The questions flowed freely, unencumbered by any inhibitions, as he sought to unravel the mysteries that lay dormant. And the viejo[10] responded in kind, sharing his recollections and experiences with candid honesty.

"When you were a child, where did you live?" -Jorge began.

"Pue[11], with papá[12] Francisco at the ranch." -replied Don Rodulfo

---

5. Desayuno Criollo: breakfast plate consisting of bread with butter, fried eggs, ham, and coffee.

6. Acerolas: wild berry.

7. Parchas: passion fruit.

8. Tamarindo: tamarind.

9. Mixta Criolla: plate served with rice, beans, meats, and some type of salad.

10. Viejo: old man used as a term of endearment.

11. Pue: way of saying the word then.

12. Papá: father.

"Was *there a lot of need there?*"

"*To el tiempo*[13]."

"*That's why you didn't go to school or learn to read and write?*"

"*My viejo needed someone's help to look after my brothers and sisters, and I was the oldest. So, I had to leave school as a child to find work and help him.*"

"*How old were you when that happened?*"

"*Maybe, six or seven. I don't remember.*"

"*Why didn't your parents live together when I was born?*"

"*My Pai[14] got drunk all the time and took all his anger out on the vieja[15]. So, she got tired of being abused and left him.*"

"*Why didn't you go with her?*"

"*I was already quite old, and she abandoned us, she did not take any of my siblings.*"

"*Not even one?*"

"*None!*"

"*And how did you meet mami[16]?*"

"*While I was visiting my vieja in Ponce, your mother lived there with her family.*"

Don Rodulfo never displayed any discomfort while responding to his son's questions. On the contrary, he met each question with a serene and genuine demeanor, a characteristic that had defined him since his son's earliest recollections. With each passing question, as breakfast was savored and the morning unfolded, Jorge found himself checking off the boxes of his list of inquiries. Time seemed to stretch, granting them a long golden

---

13. To el tiempo: jíbaro way of saying "all the time".

14. Pai: slang for "dad".

15. Vieja: old woman used as a term of endearment.

16. Mamí: slang for "mom".

opportunity to delve into the depths of a life marked by almost complete separation. As the noon hour approached, a sense of purpose enveloped them both. There was still something left to be done, a task awaiting their attention, and they were attired appropriately for the occasion.

Once again and in what seemed like an instant, they found themselves riding in Jorge's vehicle. Silence permeated the car as they resumed their journey, devoid of conversation according to Jorge's predetermined mental itinerary. Yet, within that silence, a profound calm enveloped both individuals, reconnecting fragments of their past lives on that very day. Despite the absence of words, he found solace in breathing the same air as his father, a simple yet profound connection. Don Rodulfo's presence provided a soothing balm, extinguishing the inner flames of torment that had plagued him for a very long time.

In the presence of his father, Jorge experienced a familiar tranquility reminiscent of his childhood, where the world's hurts could only be assuaged in the embrace of loving parents. His father's unique presence bestowed upon him a sense of peace he had long yearned for. It was almost unbelievable that he now had the opportunity to feel such solace. True to his plan, he resolved not to squander a single minute of that day, as he had awaited this divine opportunity for years. Following the silent journey, the two men reached their destination; a lake that held a connection to their shared hometown. Stepping out of the car, Jorge made his way to the trunk, retrieving a remarkable fishing rod that appeared to be the most exquisite in the world. It was a carefully chosen gift, knowing that his father had always yearned for such luxury, but had never been able to afford it due to a life of eternal financial constraints.

With this prized possession in hand, Jorge approached his father, Don Rodulfo, with anticipation evident in his eyes. Presenting the fishing rod, a surge of emotion overwhelmed the old man, visibly moving him to tears. He gingerly accepted the gift, clutching it tightly within his weathered hands. Jorge, fighting back his own tears, embraced his father once more, their connection strengthened by the exchange. In those precious moments, everything unfolded exactly as he had envisioned, his plan flawlessly coming to fruition. Dressed as fishermen, the two men descended a hill that led from the road to the shores of the lake. Memories of Jorge's childhood's fishing trips flooded his mind, though there were notable differences in the circumstances and motivations. In his recollections, those journeys involved traversing paths, shortcuts, and dusty roads, navigating through roads, ravines, and dirt tracks. The purpose of fishing back then held dual significance; it not only provided sustenance for the family amid poverty, but it also served as a means of generating income by selling the catch to alleviate their immediate need for cash.

However, this day unfolded differently, aligned with Jorge's meticulous plan. Economic necessity no longer drove him to fish; that chapter belonged to the past. He had achieved a certain level of success in his life, and his current need was more spiritual than material. It was a yearning that could only be fulfilled by the presence of his father in his life, and nothing would hinder him from answering the list of questions etched deep within his soul on this day. Not even the allure of wealth could entice him to forsake the opportunity to spend every precious minute on Don Rodulfo's side.

Bathed in warm sunlight, the day unfolded with a gentle breeze that kept the heat at bay. Positioned under the comforting shade of a flamboyán[17] tree by the water's edge, the two men casted their fishing lines into various sections of the lake. As the hours passed, the focus of their conversation shifted to Jorge's formative years, delving once more into his childhood. Uninhibited by any restraints, he fearlessly posed more questions to his father, seeking further insights, and understanding of the events that made him who he was:

"Why did we have to sell so much of the fish we caught?" -Jorge asked.

"To make some chavos[18]." -responded Don Rodulfo.

"Where did you work when I was born?"

"In <u>Obras Publicas</u>[19] cutting grass, but <u>me botaron</u>[20] when the economy faltered."

"Then what did you do?"

"I found little jobs here and there."

"What about aluminum cans? Why spend so much time picking them up across town?"

---

17. Flamboyán: a tree with red flowers that bears no fruit.

18. Chavos: slang for money in P.R.

19. Obras Públicas: Public Works, government agency.

20. Me botaron: they fired me.

"The aluminum cans were a way to make some chavos, so you and your siblings didn't go hungry."

"But they were almost worthless."

"They were a resuelve[21] for those times. The important thing is that we survived."

"Yes, we did survive."

"At least you didn't have to leave school and repeat my childhood."

"I know. Thank God those times were not the same."

"Amen to that!"

"Viejo, do you remember when we went to the beach with Papá Francisco?"

"Of course, my viejo loved the sea."

"We also loved the beach back then."

"Do you also remember when you punished me for cursing the neighbor out?"

"Sure, <u>las personas mayores se respetan</u>[22]."

"And do you remember when my first child was born?"

"When you turned me into a grandfather? Yes, I do remember."

"Papí are you proud of me?"

"Yes, I am. You progressed and became someone better than me."

"Don't say something like that. It's not true."

"Sure, it is. You became better than me and that is all I wanted for you and your brothers and sisters."

In the same manner, as during their breakfast conversation, Don Rodulfo responded to each question with a candid lack of inhibition, his face adorned with a gentle smile. This reaffirmed Jorge that the day was un-

---

21. Resuelve: way of saying short term solution.

22. las personas mayores se respetán: The elders are to be respected.

folding exactly as he had planned, an ideal day he had yearned for endlessly. Throughout the day, the fish seemed eager to take the bait, willingly falling into the trap of their hooks. The two men found themselves reeling in a bountiful catch, even capturing some of the largest fish known to exist. The extraordinary stroke of luck they experienced seemed inexplicable, leaving them in awe of the remarkable turn of events. Time, once again, seemed to slow down, defying comprehension. For Jorge, whose adult life had been consumed by the pursuit of wealth, this day held immeasurable value. It served as an opportunity to make amends for the lost years, during which false pride, unexplained frustrations, or sheer ignorance had driven a wedge between him and his parents for over two decades.

Gazing at Don Rodulfo, lost in his own thoughts, Jorge became acutely aware of the toll that time had taken on him. He could sense the weariness etched into his father's features, a testament to a life filled with sacrifices and hard work. Nevertheless, nothing would hinder him from placing a checkmark on each one of the boxes of his list of questions. With the arrival of evening, the sun gracefully descended upon the horizon, casting a warm golden glow. Despite the passing hours, the old man radiated youthful energy and exhibited an unwavering spirit. Satisfied with their plentiful catch, both men agreed to conclude their fishing expedition and sought a place to eat.

"What do you want to eat?" -Jorge asked.

"Anything you want." -answered Don Rodulfo.

"Today, I'm going to take you to eat seafood, a ten-pound lobster in garlic and butter, garlic shrimp or a sea scallop in sauce. Whatever you want, viejo, there is nothing you ask for in what I will not please you today!" -Jorge had rehearsed those words for a long time and had finally had a chance to use them.

"That is a desperdicio[23] of money. Please don't spend that much on me."

Jorge found himself momentarily flustered, caught off guard by the unexpected response. Embarrassment washed over him, as this particular situation had not been accounted for on the mental checklist, he had meticulously crafted. However, just as he had experienced countless times during his childhood, his father came to his rescue, rescuing him from the momentary embarrassment:

---

23. Desperdicio: waste

"What about the Lechonera[24] ?" -asked Don Rodulfo with serenity in his eyes.

In that moment, Jorge found himself contemplating the stark contrast between his own life and that of his father. He reflected on the extent of the changes and transformations that had shaped his own journey, as well as the stark differences in their respective lives. One was trapped in an eternal pursuit of material wealth and luxury, while the other remained bound by the shadows of past poverty. They stood as two individuals, separated not only by the passage of time but also by the distinct experiences that had shaped them.

After a short drive, they arrived at the lechonera that prominently displayed a succulent lechón asado[25] in its showcase, its skin appearing perfectly crispy and inviting. Beside it, a variety of delectable side dishes filled another display. Jorge ordered an abundance of food for three, even though there were only two. In his mind, it was better to have leftovers than to run out of food. As the saying goes, "Pa'que falte, que sobre"[26] . Don Rodulfo wore an expression of pure joy, emanating an aura of understanding and harmony. A profound sense of peace enveloped him, defining his demeanor on this remarkable day. Everything unfolded seamlessly, following the meticulously planned sequence of events. Jorge continued with his line of questioning, and once again, his father responded with calmness and ease, as he always did.

"How are you feeling these days?" -Jorge asked.

"I'm fine. A little bit of achaques [27], but I'm fine." -repeated Don Rodulfo.

"How have you been all these years?"

"A little bit lonely since your mom died, but I'm well overall."

"Do you need help with anything?"

---

24. Lechonera: establishment where the main dish is roasted pork.

25. lechón asado: Roasted Pig.

26. "Pa'que falte, que sobre": "better to have more than needed to not having enough".

27. Achaques; slang for "aches".

"No, I don't need ná[28]."

"Papí[29], how can I help you?"

"I don't need ná. If I need something, I will let you know."

As the night fell, Jorge felt a deep sense of satisfaction knowing that he had checked off almost every box on his list of questions. Content with the perfection of the day, filled with spiritual peace and a newfound sense of calm, he offered to drive his father back home. Boarding the vehicle, they embarked on the familiar journey, enveloped in serene silence and the comforting presence of one another. He kept his gaze straight ahead, focusing on the feeling of security that his father's presence brought him, shielding him from the world's troubles. Throughout that perfect day, he had managed to address every question that had troubled him, except for one. Having spent an entire day devoted to his old man after years of sporadic contact, he had nourished his soul with love and found profound spiritual tranquility. But there was still one lingering question, one he may not have dared to ask until now. As they approached their destination, a sense of finality hung in the air. Stepping out of the car, they shared another heartfelt embrace, wordlessly, for a full minute. It was at that moment that the man, driven by an overpowering need for closure, finally posed the question that had remained unasked:

"Papí, tú me perdonas?[30] " -asked Jorge with his heart full of hope.

In that fateful instant, Don Rodulfo's expression shifted, filled with anguish and sorrow. His eyes reflected a profound pain as if the weight of the question had shattered his soul. He gently released himself from his son's embrace, his face etched with a mix of vulnerability and hurt. With a heavy heart, he turned away, slowly retreating into the shelter of his home, leaving his son standing there, struck by the sudden despair that had enveloped his father. Then Don Rodulfo closed the door and turned off the lights.

Jorge's half-opened eyes were pierced by a sliver of light, instantly rousing him from his slumber. Outside, the day was draped in a shroud of rain and coldness. Aching in his chest, he struggled to draw a breath. Regret enveloped him, as tears failed to alleviate the profound emptiness that

---

28. Ná: slang for "nothing".

29. papí: slang for "dad".

30. ¿Papí, tú me perdonas? Dad, do you forgive me?

gnawed at his being, the hollowness of remorse. Once again, his dreams had summoned his departed father, who had passed away five years prior. Once again, his imagination deceived him, presenting him with a divine opportunity to address unanswered questions. His soul roamed the realm of dreams, yearning for connection, desperately attempting to purchase with wealth what could never be bought, an elusive few more minutes of life with his late father. Each dream plunged him deeper into the abyss of disappointment and guilt, the dagger of remorse piercing his core. Every symbolic gesture he offered on those mystical, idealized days spent with his father only fueled panic, confusion, disillusionment, sadness, and despair. The moments he yearned for in his dreams were irretrievable, forever lost. And each time, the dream concluded in the same manner: the door slammed shut, leaving him standing alone, his father withholding the answer that tore at his soul. This recurring event, etched into his subconscious, emphasized the irrevocable truth, no one could quench the burning flames of his private hell, for the remainder of his days. And that perfect day, conjured by his dreaming mind, served only to remind him that he had fallen short as a son, substituting love with material indulgence and ambition. It was a reproach, a reminder that time could not be reclaimed, nor forgiveness sought, for from the silence of the grave, death does not offer second chances.

THE COMMANDMENTS

I T WAS A VERY serene afternoon when Efrain left his house to go to church. He would walk from one side of the neighborhood to the other to get there. This was the day to praise God and offer Him some of the time He had gifted him, just like his life. He was dressed in his best Sunday clothes: a long-sleeved shirt, formal pants, and a pair of shoes clean and freshly polished. Everything looked its best to be pleasing in the presence of God. During the journey, Efrain was immersed in his divine thoughts about how happy he was in God's hands and for everything he did to live according to His will.

A few minutes after starting his trip to church, Efrain encountered a stray dog. It was dirty and mistreated and looked very hungry. The dog was scavenging for food, thrusting the contents of a garbage can, trying to find something to help him survive just one more day. For some reason that displeased the devout man. He thought about how ugly the animal looked and made violent gestures to shoo the dog out of his sight. The frightened animal tried to run to the other side of the street and didn't realize there was a car coming down the road. The driver hit the brakes, but it was a little too late, and the stray dog met its end under the wheels of the car. Efrain looked at the dead dog and thought it was better that way, so it wouldn't be dirtying the world with its ugly appearance. Besides, <u>Dios sabe lo que hace</u>[1] and works in mysterious ways. For some reason, that stray dog had to die that day, and Efrain had no right to question God's will.

---

1. Dios lo que hace: God knows what He does.

A few minutes after the dog incident, Efrain passed by a religious propaganda banner featuring an image of a white Christ with straight hair and blue eyes. It was the perfect image of the Savior according to the taste of the one who adjusted the story to sell it to an European population. On a bent knee, he paid homage to that false image of the Son of God. He thought about the beauty of that image of a white Christ and felt offended when he remembered watching a man on the television having an argument with another person about Jesus' origins. The man on the show argued that based on the geographical location of Israel and what was known of the inhabitants of the area, there was no chance Jesus would be a white man. Efrain recalled that story as he passed by his preferred version of God and thought that a brown or black Jesus wouldn't make any sense. After all, he thought, no one would be willing to pay reverence to the abomination that a dark Jesus or God would be. His Lord was a white God, as the white man had intended many centuries ago.

Further, along his path, he spotted a couple walking on the other side of the street. His neighbors Jose and his wife Raquel seemed to be walking back home from the market. While the couple walked away, Efrain couldn't help to admired his neighbor's wife body and allowed himself to dream for a moment about receiving the warmth of her most intimate affections inside the intimacy of her bedroom or elsewhere.

Efrain observed his neighbor's wife and imagined himself in Jose's place. He thought about how beautiful Raquel was and that maybe he deserved her pleasant company. After all, he was a decent, hardworking, and religious man. What more could that beautiful woman desire from her man? He thought about the things he would do to her, and what she would do to him in the privacy of their imaginary bedroom; and lust overcame him for a couple of minutes of furtive thoughts. Lost in those secretive thoughts, he continued walking to his church. Afterward, he encountered one of his biological brothers, David, who greeted him as usual:

"Where are you going, Efrain?" -David asked.

"To attend church as always." -Efrain replied.

"Hey, after going to church, are you visiting los viejos[2]?"

"Which viejos, my viejos?"

"Of course, who else would I be talking about?"

---

2. Los Viejos: the folks or elders.

"You know I haven't talked to my viejos in a long time."

"You're still on that shit about your viejos not being good enough for your Christian faith?"

"It's just that our <u>viejos viven en el mundo</u>[3] and I just can't agree with that."

"<u>Predicas la moral en canzoncillos.</u>[4] Why do you go to church then, to <u>calentar el asiento</u>[5] ?"

"My relationship with my God is paramount; please don't meddle in that because my God understands."

"I guess He is the only one that understands that nonsense you do."

"Could you stop, please? I don't want to stop talking to you."

"Fine, I'll stop asking you to do what's right, even when you should know that you're wrong."

And with that, Efrain bid farewell to his brother David to continue his way to God. Just then, he looked down and saw a man's wallet on the ground. He bent down, opened it, and saw that there was a significant sum of money inside. He searched inside for some identification but found none. He thought it was a blessing from God, so he took the money out of the wallet and placed it in his billfold; then tossed the lost wallet aside and continued his slow walk to the church. A few moments later, he came across his neighbor Juan who was searching for something around the area. The neighbor approached him and asked:

"Brother Efrain, have you found a wallet on the road?"

"A wallet on the road?"-Efrain responded with a question.

"Yes, it's brown and had all my earnings for this week inside."

"Well, I think I saw a wallet lying there by the roadside, but I didn't check it."

---

3. Viven en el mundo: way of saying " they live in sin"

4. Predicás la moral en canzoncillos: Common saying "You preach morals on your uderwares.

5. calentar el asiento: to warm up the seat, without faith.

Efrain told Juan while pointing in the direction where he had thrown the wallet. The neighbor ran towards the spot and picked up the wallet from the ground, only to find it empty. Then he returned to Efrain looking more preoccupied than upset, and asked:

"Brother Efrain, did you see anyone walking around here as you were walking up the road?"

"No, there was no one." -Efrain replied.

"Are you sure you didn't see anyone?"

"I swear to God, I didn't see anyone."

"¡Coño![6] *I lost my wallet, and I'm left with nothing for the week."*

"Maybe someone passed by here before me." -lied Efrain.

"And who could have found my money?"

"Maybe those kids from down the school. You know they walk around there causing trouble."

"I'm screwed; I lost the money for groceries. And I won't get paid again for the next two weeks."

"Have faith, brother; God doesn't forget anyone". -Efrain preached as he bid farewell to David.

David stayed there, worried about his sudden financial need, and Efrain resumed his journey to the house of God, thinking that he would offer a better offering today for the luck of having found some money with no owner. After all, how could he have known that the money truly belonged to David if the wallet had no identification? A few minutes later, he stopped to greet Pedro, one of his best friends, and stood in front of his house.

"Pedro, my brother, where are you?" -Efrain called.

"Here I am, Efrain, ¡Jodio pero no es tu culpa![7] *"* -Pedro replied.

---

6. Coño!: Damn it

7. !Jodio pero no es tu culpa!: local saying: "messed up but it's not your fault".

"Damn you man! With all the ways God has blessed you."

"He has blessed me economically, but I still have a lot of problems from all sides."

"I wish I had a beautiful house like yours, a new car like yours, and nice furniture. What are you complaining about, man?"

"What good is having all this if I don't have good health? To el tiempo enfermo[8] ."

"You know what you must do? Ask God for health, and He will bless you with health."

"I've always asked Him that I may enjoy good health, but nothing."

"You must have more faith, brother."

"Maybe what you're saying is true. Do you really think so?"

"I don't think so, I know so, Pedro. We must pray to God with faith. Okay, I'll see you later; I'm running late for church."

"Okay. Pray for me when you go to church."

"I will my friend, I will."

Efrain had already said goodbye to his friend when he started thinking about how ungrateful Pedro was; because if he had all those material things his friend possessed, he would be happy. Momentarily, that thought turned into envy. Why were there people like that who didn't appreciate anything? he wondered. After all, he had dedicated his life to God with all the sincerity in the world, and he didn't even have half of what his friend owned, and he wasn't complaining as much. In his envious reasoning, he forgot that Pedro had been suffering from many illnesses since he was a young man.

Nearly at his destination, Efrain stumbled, and in trying to regain his balance, he dropped the Bible he was carrying under his armpit. He felt annoyed with himself for letting the Word of God touch the ground. He immediately picked up the book, closed it, and placed it back under his arm, where it belonged. He arrived at the temple and greeted all his brothers in Christ. The service began at six p.m., like every Sunday. Efrain

---

8. To el tiempo enfermo: sick all the time.

jumped, sang, and praised the Lord, along with everyone else there. He felt happy and perfect in the presence of his God. He opened the Bible, tainted by all his sweat and sins, and read what the pastor asked him to read, praised as the pastor instructed him to praise. He offered a generous offering to God. When the worship was about to end, he closed his Bible, and it would be closed until the next Sunday. Then he knelt to pray to God directly. And like every Sunday, Efrain thanked God for the blessings in his life. Most important of all, he had to remind himself that a man like him was the living example of what it means to be a perfect Christian, because no one like him lived every minute of every day practicing and respecting the Ten Commandments.

 Anthills

T HE SKY WAS PARTLY cloudy, and the clouds were beginning to gather as if to discuss what was about to transpire down on the land that they oversaw. Maybe they already knew the plan for the day and were about to shed their tears over the mountains, which were covered in the greenery that always enveloped them. Landscapes waiting to be watered by the rainy blessings that the clouds seemed to offer to the dry lands of that Puerto Rican town. Down on the ground in the middle of the batey[1], a five-year-old girl was playing with a rag doll, as was common in the poor houses on the Island. The girl was having a conversation with her toy, discussing the day's itinerary. On the one hand, she had to fulfill her mother's orders: *"I don't want to see you inside the house all day"*, her mother had told her. On the other hand, her father had a different set of instructions for her that she didn't fully understand: *"Make yourself invisible"*. According to the girl's account to the rag doll, her parents were busy doing something important, and while her siblings were helping them, she was confined to stay alone in the batey without bothering anyone; especially her parents, whom she always perceived as too angry for no apparent reason.

When noon arrived, the girl's father appeared with a carreta[2] pulled by a horse. The excited girl ran toward her father to see the tired and thirsty animal with some amazement as is normal for a child that age. As her father saw her approaching, he gave her a stern look, one of those looks that convey a thousand warning words, without the person having to say one.

---

1. Batey: front yard.

2. Carreta: wagon

The girl, upon noticing her father's serious and unrelenting look, recoiled with intense fear, as she remembered the last time, he had looked at her this way and the consequences she suffered for not being able to read these expressions. Once again, alone in the batey, the little girl confessed to her rag doll that her father wasn't very nice to her, and maybe it was because she behaved badly. Even though she seemed aware that her siblings were treated differently, for some reason that treatment eluded her, she didn't receive the same kind of care.

At that precise moment, the atmosphere wasn't hot like most days, quite the opposite, it felt cool, as the clouds in the sky continued their morning fuss and prevented the sun from seeing what was happening in that neighborhood. Throughout the morning, the parents and the oldest children had worked diligently together, emptying the rancho[3] where they lived, to move to another place far from that neighborhood, in search of liberation from their greatest sorrows of poverty. By mid-afternoon, the carreta was loaded with the family's meager belongings and prepared to carry their poverty from one neighborhood to another on this specific day. Ready to leave, mom and dad gave their children directives on how to behave during this memorable odyssey and the consequences of not following their instructions to the letter.

That's how the move began, the father sitting at the front of the carreta, guiding the horse along the arid road that connected different neighborhoods with the main road, a dirt path built by the government to connect cities and towns. The sun, still hidden behind the clouds, began to descend on the cloudy horizon as the carreta continued its traveling along the royal road to another dirt path, amidst the greenery of plains and mountains, taking this poor family to their uncertain destination. At the back of the carreta, the woman made sure the children stayed seated as instructed. They sat in the middle, along with sacos[4] of clothes that served as makeshift mattresses for this uncomfortable journey. Some of them had fallen asleep, while others remained awake observing nature around the road. Everyone was hungry and everyone, except the little girl and her rag doll, was feeling tired from the arduous preparation for the move. They had placed her at the back of the cart, without considering that she was the youngest of the bunch. This action would have seemed inexplicable to anyone, but for some reason, it didn't matter to her parents.

---

3. Rancho: shack

4. Sacos: sacks

The horse pulled the carreta slowly since the load was a bit too heavy, even for a strong cart horse, but it was all the man could afford, a carreta and an old horse. In the slowness of the journey, the girl fell asleep, holding her rag doll as she used to do at home when she was sent to bed alone in the darkest corner of the rancho. The night was approaching, and the horse had stopped for a well-deserved rest. After about twenty minutes of stillness, the man climbed onto the carreta and lashed the horse, urging it to stop idling and push forward. The horse responded abruptly as it tried to escape from the pain of the whip. In the commotion, the little girl fell off the carreta and stood up frightened, feeling immense pain in her ribs. She was still asleep when she fell to the ground, her tiny body absorbing the impact without warning. And that's how the girl started crying. It was a bit dark, and in that darkness, she couldn't see the cart or her parents. Panic flooded the girl's mind, and she began to run and scream in the opposite direction of the cart. From a distance, hidden by the darkness of the night, the man and the woman looked at each other; they glanced at their other children to make sure they were asleep, exchanged a faint smile, and continued the road, listening as the distance muffled the screams of horror from the little girl they had been planning to abandon for some time.

Meanwhile, on the road, the girl, overwhelmed with fright, screamed hysterically, alone in that dark forest. Unexpectedly, the clouds started to weep; as they had been laden with emotion all morning, and the girl's cries were like the last straw they could bear. The girl sought refuge under a tree, trying to prevent the drops that would have once sent her playing in the middle of the batey, from bathing her now in the gloominess and coldness of the night. Suddenly, the chicharras[5] started to scream, as their homes had been soaked by the rain. An owl shared its grievances from a perch in a tree, and the frogs from an adjacent river began celebrating the blessed rain with loud croaks. The terrified girl invaded by the sudden fear wet herself in her semi-damp dress and continued searching for any sign of the direction her parents had taken. Among paths and thickets, she spent all her energy and sat down at the roots of a mango tree to rest. And amid cries of fear and the exhaustion of trying to find her way, she fell asleep.

The next day, the girl woke up feeling like she was in the middle of a fire, her body stinging from hundreds of different burning sensations. These fires were the result of hundreds of ant stings from an anthill located at the roots of that mango tree. Once again, screams of distress echoed along the road as the girl desperately tried to rid herself of the insects that were attempting

---

5. Chicharras: cicadas

to devour her flesh. She threw herself onto the ground, damp from the previous night's rain, and rolled in the mud. Covered in dirt, she couldn't escape the pain caused by all the bites she had received. Amidst such agony, the girl still searched for reasons why her parents hadn't come back for her. Could it be that they hadn't noticed she had fallen? In her mind, she pondered the possibility that her parents hadn't realized she wasn't with them. And no matter how much she searched for a reason, she couldn't comprehend why her parents didn't look for her.

By around ten in the morning, the girl had scratched herself so much that her nails were bloody; the itchiness from her countless welts wouldn't let her breathe without reminding her of the ant colony that had tried to devour her alive. Amid this desperation, hunger pangs struck, and she started feeling strong cramps in her stomach, prompting her to walk backward in search of the mango tree where she had fallen victim to the ants. When she reached it, she began searching the ground for a ripe mango to alleviate her hunger. Almost immediately, she found one on the ground and started eating it. In front of that tree, far from the road, the girl waited while eating mangoes, as she was sure her parents would come back for her. Three o'clock in the afternoon arrived, and the little girl began to feel chills. She was burning up with a fever. She started sobbing in the middle of the forest and shouting for her parents. *"Mamí[6], papí[7], I'm here, come find me! Help me, mamí; I'm scared! Papí, I'm here, search for me! I didn't want to fall, please don't leave me here!"*

After a few hours, the fever gained the upper hand, and the girl lay down in the grass to rest. It was then that she began to hallucinate. She was being burned by two hells—the hell of the insect bites that had turned into welts and the hell of the fevers. Slowly, she sank deeper into uncontrollable fatigue and started moaning weakly, sprawled on the damp grass. She was covered in mud, smelling of urine, with a thousand ant bites, and to top it all off, mosquitoes began to bite her all over her body. At that moment, the pain, desperation, and uncertainty had taken a toll on the little girl, and her body was surrendering to exhaustion and fever. There on the ground, she let out a silent cry while still calling for her mother: *"Mamí, it itches! Mamí, it hurts! Mamí, help me!"*

At that precise moment, a man named Erasmo was walking along the road toward his home. He was walking along the edge of the trail to avoid soiling his shoes when a particular object caught his attention in the middle of

---

6. Mamí:slang for "mommy".

7. Papí: slang for "daddy".

the path. There lay a dirty and beaten, wet rag doll. Erasmo stopped to examine the toy and realized it couldn't have been there for more than a few hours. After a few minutes, he decided to continue his way, thinking about the poor child who had lost her doll. He lowered his gaze to the ground and resumed his steps. Suddenly, he stopped when he noticed footprints in the mud where he was walking, the footprints of a child who seemed to have walked in different directions. Apparently, these footprints were recent. Erasmo paused to observe the direction the footprints were heading and to analyze if there was anything unusual about them. For a few minutes, he searched the area but couldn't see anything, only the rag doll and footprints. That's when he decided to continue walking toward his destination and erase the false premonition that had invaded his mind.

After walking for a few minutes, Erasmo suddenly stopped as his heart skipped a beat when he heard a faint moan coming from somewhere near the road. He frantically searched for the origin of those moans but couldn't pinpoint where they came from. He momentarily paused, waiting for another sound from the creature. And again, another moan sent him running towards the river, causing panic as he contemplated the fatal possibility of a small child falling into its waters. He reached the water's edge but couldn't see anything. He looked north and south of the river, from one bank to the other, but found nothing. Nerves were getting the better of him when he stumbled upon the girl, lying on the muddy ground, reeking of urine, covered in welts, and delirious with fever.

Erasmo immediately picked up the girl and, without worrying about dirtying his shoes, started running toward his home. The girl no longer had the strength to call out; she only moaned in pain. In about thirty minutes, he reached his home, where his wife, Hortencia, looked at him in astonishment. He told her how he had found the girl in the mud while she undressed the little girl, and he went to heat water on the patio's fogón[8] . As Hortencia undressed the girl, tears began to fall down her face as she saw that the girl's little body was covered in hundreds of infected insect bites. While the water was heating up, she took a cloth, dampened it, and started wiping the mud off the girl's legs and hands. After a few minutes, Hortencia gave the girl a warm bath while she still lay delirious with her fevers.

Erasmo and Hortencia laid the girl on an old catre[9] they had in one empty room, and it was there that the woman began to treat the girl's welts with alcanfor[10] and miel[11] . This home remedy was typical in the area, and

---

8. Fogón: wood stove

Hortencia applied it to the girl as she fought against the high fever and the burning sensation without opening her eyes. Hortencia prayed for the girl while lighting candles to a Catholic saint and asking for a miracle. Erasmo sat in the living room, visibly angry and worried. Noticing her husband's apparent frustration, she sat beside him to provide consolation. He told her how he had found the little girl next to the river covered in mud and insect bites. *There are some despicable people out there!* Erasmo told his wife while clenching his fists in anger. *How could they do this to such an innocent child?* A few feet away, the girl battled with the welts and fever, enveloped in the scent of honey and camphor, while the woman and her husband looked on uneasy for her safety the way her parents were supposed to.

In the evening, the couple asked themselves more questions as they watched the child struggle with the swelling of the welts and the fever that was finally starting to decrease a bit. Throughout the afternoon, Hortencia had spent her time applying alcohol-soaked cloths to the girl's forehead while reapplying the remedy for the bites. That's how they spent the night, with the girl gradually returning to her normal temperature, and the couple taking care of her on her first day of becoming an orphan with living parents. When she finally opened her eyes, the child looked around with tentative fear, but for apparent reasons the little girl knew she was safe; however, she missed her siblings more than her biological parents. Above all, she missed her rag doll, her best friend in the lonely world she lived in, with her family. Recalling what little she could remember in those precise moments, she cried out looking for her only companion, the rag doll.

As the days went by, the girl began to recover from her brief illness; although, her body bore many marks from the welts and from scratching herself to try to relieve the horrendous itching that accompanied her since she fell asleep next to the anthill. Hortencia carried on with taking care of the young girl and every afternoon she reapplied the alcanfor and miel remedy to help alleviate the bothersome irritating sensation that made the girl want to scratch. Meanwhile, Erasmo continued asking around the neighborhood if anyone knew of a mother who had lost a girl, but he found no one who answered affirmatively. After a few weeks of searching, the couple decided to look after the girl, who called herself Jesuita. And that was the name by which her adoptive parents would come to know her.

Months passed, and Jesuita still felt empty, as she still carried the void of abandonment. Although her new parents treated her well unlike her biological parents, she still missed her siblings and her rag doll. Over time, the couple grew accustomed to being adoptive parents and offered the girl the love and affection she had never experienced in her previous life. They taught her to read and write, just like they did with their grown-up children. They scolded her when she needed scolding and hugged her when she needed a hug. The girl from the road had become the girl of the house.

A year later, while Jesuita and her new dad were at the <u>plaza del mercado</u>[12] buying some viandas[13] , she caught sight of a figure that seemed familiar, and without hesitation, she ran towards the child and hugged him tightly. Erasmo was surprised when he saw Jesuita embracing the other child and both crying jumping up and down. He immediately understood what was happening and was filled with compassion, but anger at the same time; then he started looking for the adult responsible for the boy. The boy was one of the girl's brothers who, between sobs, hugs, and kisses, expressed how much he missed her. After a few minutes, Jesuita's father appeared in front of her, and the girl looked at him in astonishment and ran towards him, trying to hug him, but he didn't allow it, shoving her hand away as she approached him with open arms.

Erasmo couldn't bear the anger any longer and confronted the man, demanding an explanation for the abandonment. The argument was intense, filled with insults like <u>"Hijos de puta</u>[14] ," "cabrones[15] ," and others, and it led to a few very intense minutes where Jesuita and her brother felt panicked and began to cry. The two men continued their argument, with Erasmo demanding an explanation and Jesuita's father refusing to offer one. As people intervened, the tension began to ease, and after that intense argument, they managed to have a somewhat civil conversation, reaching a somewhat cordial agreement. When their conversation ended, Erasmo took Jesuita by the hand, and her father took her brother in the same manner, heading towards their respective homes. The two children didn't understand what was happening and started crying loudly once again. Nevertheless, the two men went in opposite directions. The two children looked at each other as much as they could, not knowing that they were also heading to different destinies.

Over the years, Jesuita maintained intermittent contact with her biological family, especially with her siblings. In her youth, as she was becoming a woman, she began to feel the resentment of being abandoned. Her adoptive parents, to whom she was eternally grateful, had given her the love and

---

12. Plaza del mercado: market place.

13. Viandas: roots like ñame, yuca, yautía.

14. Hijos de puta: sons of bitches

15. Cabrones: assholes

affection she had never received from her biological parents. However, she resented that, like her rag doll, she had been abandoned in the darkness of that road. She still had the scars from the ant bites, as a reminder of that event that faded a little in her memory. Her adoptive parents refused to give her the reasons her biological parents had offered, which left her with a sense of emptiness, resentment that couldn't be explained, and hatred she couldn't forgive.

That's how Jesuita began to resent her siblings and tried to distance herself from them forever. After all, she was just a dirty rag that was abandoned on the road. Nevertheless, they managed to maintain occasional contact throughout the years. In this way, the family that had abandoned her became her second family, which she treated with respect and eventually accepted. As the years passed, maturity taught Jesuita that her siblings had nothing to do with her abandonment; they were just children too. It was with that understanding that she managed to free herself from the resentment and hatred that consumed her since childhood and began to learn to forgive things that seemed unforgivable.

Over time, having distanced herself from those experiences of abandonment and uncertainty, she formed her own family. For obvious reasons, she always fiercely protected her children, never letting any of them fall from the carreta of her love. She learned from her mother Hortencia, to be the woman her biological mother never was, and she taught her children the lessons her adoptive parents had taught her. Jesuita always shared with her family how she had been abandoned on that dark road that evening and the terror she experienced at that moment. She always showed them the scars left by the ant bites on her body and never stopped repeating the story of how she was cured with alcanfor and miel. Granting she never learned the reasons for that abandonment, lingering in the past wasn't something she was willing to do.

Many years later, in the twilight of her life, her biological father ended up living at her home, and she welcomed him as if nothing had happened. Her children couldn't understand why she insisted on taking care of this individual who had abandoned her when she was just a child. And he, in turn, never revealed the reason for the abandonment. Her adoptive parents, Erasmo and Hortencia, had already passed away at that time. They had never disclosed the reasons given by that man. Throughout the years, they had only said that "solo Dios sabe lo que hace[16]", and that was always their only response to her insistent questions. Jesuita cared for

---

16. Dios sabe lo que hace: God knows what he does.

her biological father as if he had been the most selfless father in the world. Seeing this, her children, who had known from childhood what he had done, reproached their mother because he wasn't worth it in their eyes. Nevertheless, she took care of him until his last moment in this world, something her children knew that he didn't deserve.

Eighty-three years later, Jesuita had already witnessed the birth of the fourth generation of her family. She was a happy old woman who showed no signs of having started life as a victim of the cruelty of abandonment when she was diagnosed with a life-ending illness. Cancer-stricken and on her deathbed, she was surrounded by her extensive family, who took care of her diligently during those difficult moments. She was accompanied by the only remaining brother, Carlos, the one who had embraced her tightly after their reunion. He held one of her hands as they both asked for forgiveness for sins that were not their own. So many years had passed since she had fallen asleep beside the anthill, and still, with the scars on her skin, the girl who had stumbled on the road was on the path to death. In those endless days, she saw her relatives come and go to enjoy her company, perhaps for the last time. At that moment her children understood why she had chosen to forgive her parents and that made them love her more than ever.

You see, sometimes in life, we step on an anthill that stings us and leaves us scarred. Sometimes those bites and that burning turn us into bitter people full of hatred and selfishness, and we make it our task to pass on these bad feelings to everyone we know. In the case of my grandmother Jesuita, the girl who fell from the carreta, the acidity of the ant bites left their marks, and every time she told us the story, her eyes filled with a pain that never left her. Nevertheless, she was an example that even when we step on an anthill that stings us and leaves us scarred, we must choose honey and its sweetness to define our essence. She showed her children and everyone who had the opportunity to share time with her, that it is easier to spread the sweetness of honey than to scatter the world with anthills of hate. And as we held her hand on the fateful night when she left us, providing her with medication to ease her pain; our pain was made more bearable because she had always taught us that the honey of the people who love you can cure all the stings of any pain, even when we sometimes step into anthills full of unexplainable or unforgettable hatred.

THE LAST DEATH

O VIDIO WAS SITTING ON a banquito[1] in the front of the iglesia[2], head down and sad. The light in the place was slightly dimmed, reflecting the atmosphere of pain that was felt there. Around this house of prayer, different people were murmuring thoughts or sharing stories. In one corner, a radio played religious hymns, while in another, there were various floral arrangements and wreaths. In the center of the iglesia, there was a casket with a woman peacefully sleeping in her eternal rest. Ovidio lifted his gaze to catch a glimpse of his deceased mother, knowing these would be his last memories of her. And with tears streaming down his face, he remembered the first time his mother had died.

That first time came without warning when he was visiting his mother, Rosa. Ovidio remembered how one weekend he went to his mother's house to check on her, as was his custom. After arriving, he opened the front door with the spare key he had and entered the living room where his mother Rosa was sitting, watching a telenovela[3] on TV.

"*¡Bendición mamí[4]!*" -Ovidio greeted her.

---

1. Banquito: bench, stool

2. Iglesia: church

3. Telenovela: Sopa opera

4. Bendición mamí: bless me mom!

"*¡Dios te bendiga mijo[5] !*"-Rosa responded.

"*What are you watching?*"

"*The novela, wait, let me lower the volume un poquito[6] .*"

Rosa turned her attention to the TV remote to lower the volume, but she seemed confused as if it were the first time, she had held the remote in her hand. Upon seeing this, Ovidio commented with a tone of sarcasm:

"*What's wrong? Did you forget how to use the remote?*"

"*I can't find the volume button.*"

"*Vieja[7] , it's the button on the left.*"

"*On the left?* -Rosa asked looking surprised."

"*Yes, vieja, on the left.*"

She still couldn't find the way to lower the TV volume and, a bit frustrated by her inability to find the elusive button, she turned to her son and said:

"*Just turn it off, I can't find the darn button.*"

"*Give it to me, I'll do it.*"

That was the first time and after that, there were several instances of sudden deaths. On one of those visits, Ovidio entered Rosa's house as usual and found a coffee pot on the stove with the liquid already dried up and a cloud of dark smoke rising to the ceiling and spreading throughout the kitchen. He turned off the stove, threw the pot in the sink, and turned on the faucet to wet it. Concerned, he went in search of his mother, whom he found sitting in the living room, seemingly visibly unaware of the smoke that had filled the kitchen. Ovidio approached her and, without greeting her, said:

"*Vieja, did you forget about the coffee boiling on the stove?*"

"*I turned it off a couple of minutes ago.*"-replied Rosa looking unconcerned

---

5. Dios te bendiga mijo: may God bless you, my son!

6. un poquito: a little bit.

7. Vieja: old woman used as a term of endearment.

"No, you didn't. I just walked into the kitchen and found the <u>olla achicharra</u>[8]."

"Ohh, I thought I turned it off."

On another occasion, he found Rosa very upset because she couldn't find her wedding ring, and visibly irritated, she told Ovidio:

"I can't find my anillo[9]."

"Which anillo are you talking about?"

"My <u>anillo de bodas</u>[10]. What other anillo I would be looking for?"

"Vieja you don't have that anillo anymore."

"What do you mean I don't have my anillo de bodas? I wear it every day!"

Ovidio looked at his mother as she continued her search, knowing that she had given the anillo to his wife years ago when he got married. He began to worry and asked her:

"Mamí, are you okay?"

"Sure, I am OK. Why do you ask that?"

"Just curious, that's all." -lied Ovidio to give himself some time to think.

So, when episodes of memory loss and confusion continued to unfold, he decided to take his mother to the doctor for a health check-up. At first, Rosa emphatically refused:

"I'm not sick, you are just imagining things." -she argued as her son insisted on a medical check-up.

"It's not about that, it's just for a check-up to make sure that everything is ok."

"What's there to check? I'm not in pain; I take care of myself, and I don't need a doctor to tell me that."

---

8. olla achicharra: Charred pot

9. Anillo: ring

10. anillo de bodas: wedding ring.

"Mami, it's just in case to be on the safe side."

"Just in case of what? I'm fine. Don't worry about it."

"That's why I want to get you checked by the doctor, so I don't worry about anything. Come on vieja do me this favor."

Over time, Rosa began to give in until she finally resigned herself to the idea of going to the doctor to please her son. During the visit, they answered many questions about family history, past events, and present occurrences. Then came the 5-word memory test and a scan in combination with other tests to help identify the cause of Ovidio's mother's memory and thinking challenges. The doctor explained the process to both and urged them to wait for conclusive results which would take some time. Ovidio and his mother returned to their respective homes to wait for an answer to the question that he had been asking himself for several months. After a week of waiting, Ovidio received the dreaded cell phone call from the doctor, delivering the diagnosis. The findings came with recommendations ranging from life to death. Ovidio was advised to have a stern talk with his mother to prepare her psychologically for the impending changes that her illness would bring. At the present time, as Ovidio remembered that fateful call, he felt someone's hands touching his shoulder. It was his wife, Ramona, asking him about his well-being at this painful moment:

"How are you feeling?" -she asked in a soft and calm voice.

"Fine, just a little tired." -he replied looking exhausted amidst the pain.

"Are you sure you're, okay? Do you need a break from all of this?"

"Yes, I'm ok; she's finally at peace."

"That doesn't mean it doesn't hurt."

"It does hurt, but there's nothing we can do. She's no longer suffering."

As he uttered these words, his mind traveled back in time and remembered one of the most difficult things for him: initiating a conversation with his elderly mother about the preparations for her funeral after he had informed her of what the medical tests had revealed. That morning, he began with a deep emptiness in his chest, worrying about the impact that his words would have on his mother's heart:

"Vieja, we need to talk." -Ovidio began with a concerned look on his face.

"Talk about what?" -Rosa asked.

"You know you're sick and we need to prepare."

"Prepare for what?"

"For the time when you can no longer make decisions."

"Mijo[11], what do you mean?"

"Your illness will progress, and you might lose the ability to care for yourself."

"Mijo, I'll get better en el nombre de Dios[12]."

"Amen to that, but I still want to prepare, just in case."

"Well, if that happens you will know what to do."

"I also want to know what you want me to do on the day that..". -Ovidio took a pause unable to utter those painful words.

"On the day I die? Don't be afraid to say it. It will happen one day or another." -replied Rosa with sincerity.

"I wish we didn't have to but, we must talk about it."

"Well, there's nothing to discuss, just bury me."

"Mamí, what do you want me to do for you?"

"Nothing, mijo. Just don't suffer because of me."

"You know that's not possible. I will miss you forever when that time comes."

"I know that, but you must be strong and understand that's God's will and nothing can change it."

"I want to know what you want me to do for you at that moment."

"Okay. I want the viewing to be held in my iglesia, and I want my pastor to deliver my Christian eulogy."

"Okay. I will arrange it with the pastor."

---

11. Mijo: slang for "my son".

12. En el nombre de Dios: in the name of God.

"I also want to buy a dress with a floral design like the one my mom had on the day we buried her. I want to look pretty like her."

"Okay mamí, we'll buy it together."

"I want my brothers in Christ to sing my favorite religious hymns, if it's not too much to ask."

"I'm sure they won't mind doing that for you."

"But above all, mijo, I don't want you to suffer when I die."

"That's not possible, it will hurt not having you in my life."

"Son, dying is part of life; the day I go, it will just be part of life."

"Even so, you can't ask me not to feel pain."

"All I'm asking is that you have peace and for you to remember that <u>Dios sabe lo que hace</u>.[13]*"*

This memory brought Ovidio back to the present and the pain he was feeling in that neighborhood's iglesia that his mother used to attend, before dying so many times. People passed by the coffin to pay their respects to the deceased woman and then approached him to offer their heartfelt condolences. Some had anecdotes or stories known to him or completely new ones.

"Your mom <u>era una santa</u>[14]*."* -a neighbor said.

"When I was younger, she helped me a lot. Gave me a lot of useful advice that I will never forget." -another neighbor commented to Ovidio who was still sitting in the banquito.

"Why do good people die?" -the first one asked in that familiar, yet nonsensical way unusual for such a serious moments.

Thus, the people continued to offer condolences in their own way, and Ovidio remained silent and listened to all the sincere attempts these people were making to ease his pain. A few minutes later, he found himself alone, and once again, he began to remember the many other deaths of his beloved

---

13. Dios sabe lo que hace: God knows what he does.

14. Era una santa: was a saint.

mother. At first, Rosa refused to leave her home, and he ended up changing his routine of visiting only on weekends. Now he would go to Rosa's house every day. Upon arrival, Ovidio would play music on an old-fashioned record player. The vinyl records sounded old with that distinctive sound of static that defined them, and some were so old that sometimes they would skip a few lines in the songs, but this was the music Rosa liked, and he got used to listening to it with her having to forgo the technology on his cell phone.

"¡Recordar es vivir![15] *."* -said Rosa on more than one occasion.

"And what does this music remind you of?" -Ovidio asked.

"Mis viejos[16]*, your father, my youth, my life..."*

"And do you remember their names?"

"Of course, my father's name was Candido, and my mom's name was..." -replied Rosa before taking a pause when she realized that she had forgotten her mother's name.

"¡Ay Dios mio![17] *I can't remember my mother's name anymore."* - she finished looking very concerned.

"Abuela[18] *'s name was Ernesta, and we used to call her mamá Nesta."* -Ovidio said to help her remember.

"Ernesta, that was her name?"

"Yes, Ernesta. That was her name. See that portrait on the wall? The one of the old woman wearing that floral dress?"

"Oh, yes! That's my mother. She loved floral dresses."

"Yes, that's your mother, abuela Nesta."

"She was a beautiful woman, wasn't she?"

---

15. ¡Recordar es vivir!: "to remember is to live."

16. Mis viejos: "my parents".

17. ¡Ay Dios mio!: Oh my God!.

18. Abuela: grandmother

"Beautiful like you mami."

"I don't want to forget them."

"You won't forget. I'll remind you whenever you need it."

"Please, don't let me forget my viejos."

"No, Mom, I'll remind you. Shall we continue with the music?"

"Yes, let's listen to my records."

Among Rosa's music collection were romantic songs, typical salsa, and sacred music. Even in her almost sound mind, she confessed to her son how these music genres revived her soul, which songs were her favorites, and which ones reminded her of her husband. On these and other occasions, Ovidio was overtaken by emotion, thinking about his father and how his sudden death on his forties had left them alone. Nevertheless, this daily contact with his mother gave him hope that the progression of the diagnosis would be slower than the doctor predicted. As the months passed, the situations and the forgetfulness began to paint a different picture than what he had hoped for. Over time, Ovidio decided to hire a neighbor to help with his mother's care. The progression of the disease dictated it. Two years had passed since that first death, and the damages of that illness were already evident.

After reminiscing about so many events in recent years, Ovidio stood up from the banquito and walked towards the coffin to look at his mother's corpse. With tears streaming down his face and the immense void he felt, he decided to leave the iglesia for a moment, to distance himself from the painful air of loss. Walking towards the door, he felt the gaze of people following him as if he were a stranger in the place. He knew that those people only wanted to show support in that difficult moment, but the pain of orphanhood is a private pain, and no one can help fill the eternal void of a loved one's death. Outside the iglesia, averting being alone was unavoidable. Moncha, his neighbor and mother's caregiver, approached him to offer her condolences with a heartfelt embrace. Before entering the iglesia to pay her respect, this kind woman took a moment to share her grief and memories with the grieving son. Then, he decided to take a short walk near the iglesia. Once again, in his solitude Ovidio's memory betrayed him, and he found himself back in the past, talking to Moncha on the phone.

"You must come right away." -Moncha said on the phone sounding a little alarmed.

"What's happening?" -he asked.

"She was a bit aggressive today and threw all her food on the floor."

"I'll be right there."

Upon arriving at the place, Ovidio entered at the precise moment when Rosa was shouting at the neighbor.

"Don't bother me, I don't know you, you damn bitch telling me what to do. Get the hell out of my house." -screamed Rosa at her caregiver Moncha.

There was a dining chair lying on the floor and spilled water from a glass, while scattered pills and some breakfast food could be seen around. The visibly concerned neighbor addressed Ovidio:

"Today, she refused to take her medication, skipped breakfast, and has been yelling and throwing things all morning. Talk to her and see if she'll listen to you."

"Okay, let me try. Thank you, I know it's not easy."

"That's nothing, you know she's like family to me."

"I know, but still. Thank you!"

The angry mother continued using vulgar words against the neighbor, and upon hearing those words, Ovidio sank into a deep sense of disappointment and concern. The doctor had warned him during one of the many visits that there could be violent or aggressive behaviors. Nevertheless, hearing Rosa who had spent her entire life in religious devotion, using those words, caused him a sharp pain and sorrow in his heart. Although he had been preparing for those moments for a while, he was never ready to face the living death of this woman who meant so much to him. Event after event, fight after fight, Rosa continued losing her mental and physical faculties, and one of those days that Ovidio had hoped would never come finally arrived. Moncha called him to help bathe his mother, as she hadn't been able to bathe alone for some time. Upon entering the house, he greeted the neighbor and headed to his mother's room. When he entered, she looked at him with surprise and a smile appeared on her face as she greeted him:

"Salvador, my love, you've returned! You don't know how much I've missed you since you left me alone. And your son, wait until he finds out that you are here again. He misses you so much, although he pretends, he doesn't. Ovidio is going to be so happy! Why did you leave us? What did we do?"

Upon hearing these words, Ovidio was filled with raw emotion and left the room with tears streaming down his face. Hearing his mother yearning for his father was a lash that his heart was not ready to receive. He missed his father, that was the truth since his sudden death many years before. The void the father had left in his son's life was impossible to fill and for that man who now, too, was a witness to the countless times his mother had died while still breathing. After a few minutes, he entered the room again, and Rosa looked at him with surprise and said:

"Mijo, why are you crying?"

"It's nothing, vieja. It's just allergies."

"Did you already say hello to your dad? He is visiting, you know. Don't waste your time like before and go and <u>pídele la bendición</u>[19]."

"Yes, I already said hello and asked for his bendición, but now you must shower."

"Yes, because I think that Salvador is taking me on a date. It's been so long."

"Maybe, Vieja, maybe. -Ovidio said trying to keep his composure."

As the days passed, Rosa's behavior became erratic and unpredictable. Some days she would shout obscenities at Moncha and even at her own son. Other times she would sob because of aches that she couldn't explain to others. Sometimes she would start moving her hands or feet as if her body was preparing to run without the rest of her. She would get lost in her own house, and on some occasions, she wouldn't sleep through the night, walking around muttering words to herself. All these symptoms were expected; yet they were very difficult for Ovidio to witness.

Finally, the day came when Ovidio and his wife decided to bring Rosa to live with them. They prepared a room and became the last witnesses of her cognitive decline. One day, he entered the room with all the medications his mother had to take in the morning. The lady lay in bed with her eyes open, staring at the ceiling. He called out to her:

"Mamí, I'm here with your medications." He said but Rosa didn't respond, her gaze fixed on the ceiling.

"Vieja, here's your medicine." -Rosa continued staring at the ceiling.

---

19. pídele la bendición: ask him for his blessing.

"Vieja, get up please." -cried Ovidio with some tears streaming down his face as the fears set in.

Then Rosa turned her head slowly to look at her son and asked:

"Who are you? What are you doing at my house?"

"I'm your son Ovidio, vieja." -replied the man with some sense of relief.

"My son?"

"Yes, your son Ovidio."

"And you're not the young man who takes care of me?"

"Yes, mamí, I'm the young man who takes care of you, Ovidio your only son."

"My only son..."

As the months went by, Rosa began to have difficulty eating, just as the doctor had predicted, thus signaling the last stages of the disease. Day after day, Ovidio and the family took turns caring for her. Even Moncha who had looked after her, came daily to assist with the daily effort. Eventually, Rosa stopped speaking and eating. The dreaded final moment was approaching, and everyone in the household prepared to say goodbye to this important figure in their family. One morning, Rosa deliriously lay in bed, Ovidio sitting in front of her since the previous night, unable to close his eyes, holding her hand. With their mutual suffering, the minutes of her life were dwindling. He silently wept in front of his mother, afraid to let her know that he was already suffering. He was resigned to the pain that her death would bring but was not ready to say goodbye. After an intense day, Rosa's body could no longer resist, and at some point, she forgot to breathe, thus marking the end of her time.

Once more standing in front of the coffin, Ovidio observed his mother, feeling a whirlwind of emotions surrounding his soul. He felt orphaned by Rosa's departure and angry about the way he had lost her. Then he felt guilty for having, at some point in his desperation, wished for his mother to find rest so that he could rest as well. Enveloped in that whirlwind of thoughts, he looked around at all the people who had gathered to accompany him during this sorrowful occasion. He felt grateful for the love and affection his mother had given him. He appreciated that his wife, the neighbor Moncha, and the entire Puerto Rican neighborhood had gifted him their company as a show of love and respect for his mother. He felt at peace. Finally, the time came to close the coffin, and that intense moment brought him to his knees, while his wife and others embraced him. Through timid sobs and loud cries, he watched as the lid of the coffin enclosed the image of that beautiful woman, taking her to her eternal rest.

Upon arriving at the cemetery, the iglesia's pastor began to speak words of mourning as the grave was filled with the earth that would bury Rosa for her eternal sleep. Ovidio standing by watched and recalled some of his mother's living deaths. And in the recounting of these living deaths, he found solace in knowing that he had done everything he could for her. And though everyone mourned her at that moment, including himself, Rosa hadn't died on that Friday as people said. She had died in life over the course of five years, as it happened when she forgot, memory by memory, event by event, breath by breath. Ovidio's mother's last death happened on the day that she had forgotten the last memory of her own life.

INSOMNIA

T HE NIGHT WAS CALM; it wasn't too cold or too hot. It was a night for a perfect sleep. The mosquitoes weren't bothering anyone who was asleep in that neighborhood in Puerto Rico. However, Margarita couldn't sleep. She had a terrible premonition that something bad was going to happen. She got out of bed and walked towards the kitchen, and with every step she took, Margarita felt the tensions of her fears and the relief of her hopes going back and forward with her movements. And no matter what she did, she still couldn't calm her rattled nerves. Then she opened the lacena[1] to search for her manzanilla[2] and dried linden[3] seeds, to boil them in water and make herself a tea that she hoped would calm her nerves a bit so she could sleep. Margarita had been suffering from maternal insomnia for years.

After making the tea, she went to sit in the living room with the lights off, feeling a sense of emptiness in her chest. Margarita, carrying that premonition, was resigned to receiving a phone call or having someone knock on her door with bad news. She took a sip of tea and another one, closed her eyes, and knelt to pray. She asked God to protect him, to open his eyes, and above all, to bring him back home alive. She begged God for her son to win the personal war he was wagging against drug abuse. And as

---

1. Lacena: cupboard

2. manzanilla: chamomile

3. Linden: tilo

an offering, she offered the rest of her life in communion with divine grace and at His complete mercy.

Sitting there with her cup of <u>Té de tilo</u>[4], Margarita thought and thought about how her son had ended up in such a situation. She closed her eyes as if to investigate the past and find out what she had done wrong. What sin had she committed to have to pay for this sentence? That's how she began to relive her son's life in sporadic thoughts that came and went like scenes from a love movie mixed with episodes of disappointment and even some horror.

"Mamá, mamá."-were the first words that her little boy, Ricardo, spoke.

A sharp memory takes Margarita back in time when the boy was running through the backyard, and she ran after him.

"Mijo[5] don't run, you'll fall."-she advised.

Another vivid memory from a few years past found Margarita with pride oozing out of her body upon hearing her son's voice.

"Mamí, my teacher says I'm in the honor group because I have all A's in my <u>tarjeta de notas</u>[6]."

Suddenly, a warm feeling crossed her cheeks bringing her back to the present. Without realizing it, Margarita was silently crying, and her tears had fallen into her tea, adding a little saltiness to its semi-sweet taste. So many beautiful memories, so many promises, and so much disappointment had kept her in that insomnia from which she couldn't free herself for a long time. Cursed fate had stolen her son's life in broad daylight, while she tried everything to bring him back to the right path. At first, Margarita tried to reason with her son and talked to him about the consequences of his actions and how they could ruin his young and promising life. Ricardo responded by denying the baseless accusations of people. Margarita proceeded to beg her son to do the right thing as a favor to her:

"Mijo, please do it for me."-she pleaded with her son.

---

4. Té de tilo: Tea to help people sleep prepared with chamomile, linden, and sugar.

5. Mijo: slang for "my son"

6. tarjeta de notas: Report card

"Vieja[7], I don't know what you're talking about." -Ricardo replied.

"You need help, professional help."

"I don't need anything, vieja, I'm fine."

"People have told me they've seen you involved in bad things."

"People always talk nonsense. Those bochincheros[8], always talking shit." -complained Ricardo visibly upset.

"Are you sure it's just people and nothing else?"

"Vieja, I'm sure, I'm not involved in anything bad. You know that people like to talk."

The reality of what Ricardo was living was obvious to his mother. After all, she had raised him and knew his character. That's why it broke her heart to see how slowly the body of her son was fading away. It wasn't just his muscles that were being lost; it seemed like he was also losing his vocabulary and expressive way of communicating. He was also losing his shame, and lying had become second nature to him. Of all the things that could have happened to her, it was this that ruined her sleepless nights. After a few minutes, the deep sense of loss that Margarita felt, didn't give her any signs of surrendering to the taste of tilo, manzanilla, and a little bit of salt from her own tears.

Margarita sat in the living room, still wrestling with her memories when she felt a hand touch her right shoulder, followed by a question from her husband Raúl:

"Why are you still awake?" -he asked, even though he already knew the answer to his question.

"I can't sleep." -Margarita replied.

"What's wrong with you?"

"I don't know where the niño[9] is?"

---

7. Vieja: old woman used as a term of endearment.

8. Bochincheros: Gossipers.

9. Niño: kid, boy

"He must be fine, doing his own thing."

"That's what worries me."

"You have to stop worrying; he's not a baby anymore. He is a manganzon[10] who should know better."

"I know, but he's sick."

"He's a sinvergüenza[11] that's what he is. It's not an illness." -commented Raúl upset.

"I know you don't see it that way, but it's an illness."

"That boy is taking advantage of us."

"I'm his mother, and all I want is to help him. I don't want anything bad to happen to him."

"He's a <u>hijo de puta</u>[12] who abuses us while he goes and gets high, and we can't even sleep because of him."

"We have to keep trying."

"If we keep going like this, you or I will get sick. We have other children and even grandchildren who need us too."

"I know, but the others are fine, and Ricardo is not."

"So, do we ignore those who do the right things and worry about the one who doesn't?"

"It's not like that. The others are fine, and they don't need us as much as he does. We have to help the one who needs us the most. The others will understand."

"I'm going to bed, <u>al carajo</u>[13] with that boy who doesn't appreciate anything we do."

---

10. Manganzon: slang for huge or big person.

11. Sinvergüenza: person who lacks a sense of shame.

12. Hijo de puta: son of a bitch

13. Al carajo: to hell with

Raúl went to the bedroom, upset, and tried to sleep while crying his fears silently so Margarita wouldn't hear him. In reality, his son's situation tore his soul apart, and he no longer knew how to help him. In moments of exasperation, he decided it was better to ignore Ricardo's problem and not get sick trying to face the harsh reality as it was. He got into bed and beneath the sheets, he silently murmured all his frustrations so that his wife wouldn't notice that his life was also dwindling away in this nightmare of having a drug-addicted son and seeing his wife Margarita spend sleepless nights waiting for a miracle or something worse.

Meanwhile, in the living room, Margarita got up from the sofa and pressed her head against the door of the bedroom, listening to her husband express everything that bothered him in a low voice. It caused her so much pain because she knew that the boy not only was like la _luz de los ojos de su papá_[14], but also the source of so much of the disappointment that he dealt with day after day. A minute later, She went to open a window, looking outside and hoping for some miracle to bring her son home. After a while, she sat back down in front of the teacup and took it in her hands to have a little more of that homemade remedy.

Suddenly, someone knocked on her door, sending a nervous shock through the woman's body, causing her to drop the teacup to the floor. She looked at the door in disbelief and terror, as she had spent the entire night with that bad premonition. The door rang again, and Margarita made efforts to walk towards it, her voice trembling with nerves and her heart sunken to the floor. She approached the door slowly and asked with a trembling voice:

"_¿Quién es?_[15] "

"_It's me, Richie._" -a voice from outside replied.

Immediately, Margarita opened the door, not giving her son a chance to take a step before she embraced him, crying. It didn't matter that the boy was disheveled, dirty, and smelled really bad. Nor did it matter that his hands bore the marks of a thousand needles due to his addiction. Her son was alive and, in her arms, and that was all that Margarita had asked of God. After that embrace, the two of them entered the house, and the confused young man looked at his mom.

---

14. La luz de los ojos de su papá: local expression: the light in the father's eyes.

15. ¿Quién es?: Who is it?

"Vieja, why are you crying?" -the young man asked.

"It's nothing, I'm just happy to see you." -Margarita replied.

"But vieja, I was here two days ago."

"I know, but you know that your dad and I always worry."

"Don't worry, I'm fine."

"Are you sure? People are saying that someone is looking for you."

"That's a lie, nobody's looking for me. Why would anyone be looking for me?"

"Mijo, that's what people are saying, and you know I worry about something happening to you."

"Nothing's going to happen to me. I know what I'm doing."

"Ricardo, why don't you come live with us?"

"You know how papi[16] is, and I don't want to argue with him."

"Your dad worries too."

"I don't think so, besides, he doesn't have anything to worry about."

"Okay, okay. Let's not fight. Are you hungry?"

"A little bit. What's there to eat?"

"Whatever you want. I could make you anything you ask for."

"Then make me a <u>pan con huevos</u>[17] sandwich."

"Will do that. Let me go make it. Go and take a shower; you're all dirty."

"But vieja!"

"No buts. Take a shower while I make you your sandwich. Look for some of the clothes you left in your room and put them on."

---

16. papí: slang for "dad".

17. Pan con huevos: bread with eggs.

"Okay, mami[18] *Is the viejo*[19] *sleeping?"*

"Yes, he went to bed a while ago."

Inside the bedroom, Raul listened to his wife's conversation with their son, experiencing a strong urge to go out, hug him, and kiss him, but he resisted. His <u>orgullo de macho</u>[20] wouldn't allow him to give an inch of honor to that troubled boy. He stood by the door and waited. He waited for his son to take a shower and waited to hear his voice a little longer. Still, he didn't leave the bedroom, refusing to give in.

Meanwhile, in the kitchen, Margarita was thrilled because it seemed that God had taken pity on her. She thanked Him because her son was there, safe, even if he wasn't healthy. She cooked what her son had requested and a little extra. She made the eggs he asked for, toasted the bread, and spread some butter on it. She cooked him bacon and made him coffee, just the way she knew he liked it. Margarita was at peace, feeling how the presence of her son relieved her worries from the previous nights. And she drifted off to a dream momentarily.

She saw a future where her son had been rehabilitated from that world of drug abuse. She saw him married with children, and she saw him working and earning his living with the sweat of his brow, not like he was doing now, stealing from the neighborhood houses to satisfy that craving of flying with his feet on the ground. Then she remembered how she, at one point, even offered money to her son to buy drugs without stealing, on the condition that he used them at home. She knew that this was not right, not even for herself, but her son's safety was more important than her pride or what people would say. Then, her thoughts were interrupted by a voice:

"Vieja, I've taken a shower already." -announced Ricardo from the living room.

"Okay, I'll bring you the food so you could sit down and eat." -Margarita replied.

Ricardo sat at the table and, without worrying about himself with proper manners, ate the bread, eggs, and bacon, and drank the coffee as if he hadn't eaten for more than three days. As he ate, Margarita watched him

---

18. Mamí: slang for "mom".

19. Viejo: old man used as a term of endearment.

20. Orgullo de macho: male pride

gratefully, thanking God that she could still see him breathe. And that's when she regretted having judged other mothers in the neighborhood who had experienced similar situations, privately labeling them as bad mothers. After a few minutes, the son finished eating and stood up from the table, moving back and forth in the dining room in an act of inexplicable desperation for anyone who had never been addicted to substances. Margarita approached him slowly:

"What's wrong mijo?" -she asked.

"Na[21] *mami', na'. I'm fine."*

"Stay in your room tonight so you can sleep well and leave tomorrow."

"I can't, vieja, I can't."

"Yes, you can. Please do it for me!"

"I'll do anything for you, vieja, but not tonight."

"But why not?" -Margarita asked in a lovely tone as if she was speaking to a child.

"I just can't; I need to do something."

"What do you have to do that can't wait until tomorrow?"

"Something, vieja, something."

"Please, mijo, stay tonight, only for one night."

"I can't tonight, vieja. I'll come tomorrow; I swear it."

-¡*Ay bendito*[22] *mijo, please!*

Finally, the desperate young man opened the front door, planted a kiss on Margarita's forehead, and left the house, disappearing into the darkness of the serene night. Leaning against the door frame, Margarita once again pleaded with God to bring her son back to her. In the room, her husband silently prayed for the same. Those two individuals were trapped in their own private hells of worry and disappointment, both suffering in their

---

21. Na': slang for "nothing".

22. ¡Ay bendito!: slang that expresses happiness, sadness, or surprise depending on the tonality of the voice

own way the slow devastation that drug abuse inflicts on the addicts and their families.

After a few minutes, Margarita closed the door of her house, and once again, that sense of worry returned to disturb her. She went to the kitchen and once more attempted to kill those sleepless nights with a mixture of manzanilla, tilo, and a pinch of salt from her own tears. Raúl emerged from his room visibly affected, asking her to lie down. He hugged her and tried to calm her, whispering sweet words in her ear. Wrapped in the warmth of that embrace and plagued by a terrible premonition, Margarita once again recalled how Ricardo had entered such a dangerous world and the anger that consumed her when she remembered that moment in the doctor's office after an unexpected bicycle accident where her son injured his back.

"I'm going to prescribe you these painkillers." -the doctor said.

"And how many do I have to take?" -Ricardo asked.

"One every eight hours."

"And for how long do I have to take them?"

"Until you feel better, then we'll see."

That was how Ricardo started using those painkillers to relieve his pain. Gradually, he became accustomed to the sensations they caused, and after using them for a few months, he couldn't imagine living without them. The doctor discontinued the use of those medications, opening the doors to substance abuse, which would lead the boy down the path of destroying his dreams and most of his life. He started buying pills on the street, and when they no longer had an effect, he turned to cocaine, and eventually, he started injecting himself.

After that, intermittent encounters with law enforcement began. He was arrested several times for stealing from grocery stores and other small businesses. This was followed by robberies in the neighborhood where he had grown up. Many of the neighbors tried to advise and help him, even after he had stolen from them, but they ended up beating him up when they caught him trying to steal from them again. His addiction was insatiable, and he stole from his family, his father Raúl, his mother Margarita, and even from his siblings. Everyone grew tired of his refusal to listen, and everyone gave up on their efforts to help him. Everyone except his mother.

In the present, Ricardo was merely a ghost of who he used to be before the accident. And it was that ghost that haunted his mother at night in her eternal state of waiting, for she was waiting for God to grant her a miracle. She was waiting for a change, and she was also waiting for a tragedy, one that she had been trying to prevent for some time. In the present, Ricardo was a victim of an accident and a doctor's malpractice. And his father Raúl was a victim of reality and his own orgullo[23]. Well past midnight, still sitting in the living room with her teacup in hand, Margarita was another victim of the tragedy of her son, as she had been suffering from maternal insomnia for years. It was the kind of insomnia no mother can escape, no matter how hard they try to appease it with a blend of manzanilla and tilo, mixed with tears of pain and a small glimmer of undying maternal hope...

---

23. Orgullo: pride

COMPADRES

T HE SUN SCORCHED THE zinc roof of the house, while the wind brought hot breezes that made the structure feel like a tin can set on fire on the inside. It was twelve noon during another eternal hot Puerto Rican summer, nothing new, as everyone living on this Island was accustomed to such temperatures. Inside the house, still, under the shield of his mosquito net, Salvo half-slept the alcohol-induced dreams of the previous night. The heat under that zinc roof began to feel unbearable, and he sweated profusely on his catre[1], trying to stay lying down for a few more minutes. The confusion about the events that had transpired on the previous night still enveloped his mind as he wondered if the recurring visual memory in his head was the result of an experience or a product of alcohol fumes still running wild in his bloodstream. Overwhelmed by that persistent memory, Salvo sat at the edge of the catre. He was semi-naked, wearing only his underwear, and he still couldn't focus his gaze as his head spun incessantly threatening to make him fall off the catre.

"¡Coño[2]! It seems like I went overboard at the barra[3] last night. Did I really do that? And why? It can't be, I've been drunk many times, but never to that extent." - Salvo said to himself.

---

1. Catre: cot

2. Coño: Danm it.

3. Barra: Bar

After a while, he got up from his catre and leaned against the wall to avoid falling. The alcohol still coursed through his body, something inexplicable for a professional borrachón[4] like him. After swaying side to side, Salvo bent down and at the edge of the catre, he found the punchera[5] he used as an emergency toilet during the night and realized that his aim the previous night hadn't been as accurate as he thought. Urine was flowing down under the bed, and he would be forced to clean it before the humidity and the heat in his room turned it into unbearable fumes of piss smell. Again, with some effort, Salvo stood up and headed to the kitchen, where he had a bucket of water and a dirty cloth that served as an improvised mapo[6]. Walking to the kitchen, he encountered his best friend, compadre Torán, in his small living room. He was sitting there with his eyes closed, almost motionless. Salvo stopped for a moment, looking confused, and then walked over to the armchair to wake up his friend.

"Compaí[7] Torán, wake up." -Salvo said, placing his hand on Torán's shoulder.

"Oh, coño, you scared me, compaí Salvo!" -Torán reacted.

"Weren't you supposed to go home last night?"

"I think so, or maybe not, truth is, I don't remember."

"Well, I thought I saw you go home last night."

"That's what I thought."

"So, why are you here at this hour? And more importantly, how did you get in?"

"I needed to talk to you, compadre, and before I leave, I think we need to talk."

"Can't wait until later?"

"I don't think so, honestly, I'm not sure." -Torán said.

---

4. Borrachón: drunkard

5. Punchera: chamber pot

6. Mapo: mop

7. Compaí: Slang for Compadre

"Tell me something, what happened last night that I can't remember that well?"

"I don't know, something happened, but it escapes my mind. For some reason I can't remember.

"We had a big argument, didn't we? -asked Salvo still confused."

"I don't remember, compaí, all I know is that I don't know how I ended up here, but I urgently need to talk to you."

"Well, I remember that we fought, and I don't know why."

"What do you remember?" -asked Torán looking rather curious.

And that's how Salvo began narrating the memory that had been bothering him all morning.

"We were at Don Tomás' barra as usual, relaxing and having palos [8] *of Palo Blanco* [9]. *You were happy; I was happy, and we were going to draw a hand of Dominoes at the table. We beat Miguel and Cheó first. You made a "capi-cú* [10] *" move, and they got upset and started arguing to avoid paying for the round of palos. We kept playing and winning against* <u>medio mundo</u> [11]. *We drank the whole night gratís;* [12] *truth is, we had never had such a good time."*

"So, why did we start arguing?" -Torán asked.

"That's what I don't remember." -Salvo replied.

The truth was that Salvo did remember, but the confusion from last night and this afternoon didn't let him shake off the doubts he had in his soul. If he was going to tell the truth, he would have to find a way to communicate it to his friend in a way that wouldn't diminish their relationship, which

---

8. Palos: slang for "shots".

9. Palo Blanco: Local rum brand.

10. Capi-cú: Domino game that results in 100 points.

11. Medio mundo: half the world

12. Gratís: for free

they had maintained since they were two poor muchachos[13] running through the neighborhood bushes. Salvo couldn't figure out how to start the conversation, so he looked for an escape by offering his friend a cup of black coffee.

"Compaí Torán, would you like a cup of <u>café puya</u>[14]?" -Salvo asked.

"Yes, give me a café puya, because this drunkenness has me confused like never before." -Torán replied.

"And something to eat? Some galletas[15] or <u>pan con mantequilla</u>[16]?"

"No, I'm not hungry right now."

"I'm going to boil some eggs to curb my hunger a bit."

"Sure, go ahead, I'll wait for you."

Salvo walked to the two-burner stove in the corner of his small kitchen. He turned on one of the burners, found an old pot he had, and filled it halfway with water from the bucket of drinking water he kept in his kitchen as he had no running water in his home. Then he put two eggs in the pot and placed it on the stove's top. While still looking at his friend sitting at the small table, he reviewed in his head the events he remembered or didn't remember from the previous night with a deep psychological pain he couldn't explain. His mind, still clouded by alcohol, replayed that senseless event.

As it happened, the previous night the two men had gone to the barra, as was their custom. There, they played dominoes and drank almost all night for free, after an inexplicable winning streak. At some point during the night, inappropriate comments were made about people living in the neighborhood, the politicians governing the country, and even the priests of the Catholic Church. Everyone in that neighborhood knew that anything was fair game at the barra, and getting upset about a comment was the sincerest display of weakness one could show, so no one dared to take offense to any inappropriate remarks. There were some arguments at the

---

13. muchachos: kids

14. café puya: slang for sugarless black coffee.

15. Galletas: soda crackers.

16. pan con mantequilla: bread with butter.

domino table as well as at the pool table about the validity of certain plays, while some borrachones[17] complained about how tough life was; some women listened to music on the vellonera[18], and even some elderly folks followed their routine of chewing tobacco. No argument caused anyone to lose their temper, so it could be said that nothing out of the ordinary had happened.

Salvo sitting at the domino table was playing like a tag team player, with his compadre Torán. Both of them had a system to communica their different domino tiles, and they were so discreet that over the years, no one had noticed how they seemed to guess the tiles each other possessed. After winning enough to drink for free, the two men said goodbye to the domino table and stood by the vellonera. They started putting money in to play songs that reminded them of one thing or another.

And the conversation, that flared up the anger and resentment between Salvo and his <u>amigo del alma</u>[19] began, as it usually does with two borrachones:

"Wow, this song reminds me of my girlfriend from some time ago." -Torán said.

"Which one of them?" -Salvo asked.

"One of the ones I loved the most in my life."

"And with so many women you've had, this one seems special."

"Yes, but some are really, really special."

"A special woman for you? Don't mess with me, compai, you just want some ass, and when you get it, you're out."

"Not always, not always."

"And what was her name?"

"I'll tell you later, compai, I'll tell you later."

---

17. Borrachones: drunkards

18. Vellonera: jukebox

19. Amigo del alma: very best friend.

The two drunk men continued listening to music and drinking as was their custom. Since they were young, both of them worked for the same company, sharing their work schedules as well as their time at the barra. They were typical men from that neighborhood, a poor place where one could observe the daily struggle against economic desperation while being inundated by political banners that offered beautiful futures if you chose the person in the portrait. While on the other hand, the church offered salvation and a better life after the ironic prerequisite of having to die first to get such rewards. That's why the most realistic relief for the people in this neighborhood was alcohol. The bartender didn't care if you were ""de la palma"[20] or "de la pava."[21] It didn't matter if you were Catholic, Pentecostal, Baptist, or a non-believer. The only religion in his barra was money, and the bartender only cared if you had a little of it. And those two friends had no faith or political affiliation, but they always had some money to drown their miseries with liquor.

Several minutes passed, and the men, completely drunk, sang along to the songs played by the vellonera and stumbled while trying to dance with their wobbly legs. Since they had won several rounds of drinks at the domino table, they still had money to keep drinking, even though their body movements were completely inhibited by all the alcohol they had consumed. The bartender watched them in front of the vellonera, making fools of themselves, and he knew that when these two were this drunk, they became reckless. That's why he calmly asked them to go to their respective homes and come back the next day.

The mental image with the bartender brought back Salvo to remember the unfortunate discussion he had with his friend. All of this was happening now, at his home, while making boiled eggs and bringing coffee to a boil for his compadre and himself. And that memory boiled in his mind, hot and uncontrollable, like the coffee boiling in the tin coffeepot, the original way his ancestors taught him to make coffee. He couldn't wait any longer and returned to the table where his compadre awaited, half asleep. Once again, he tapped his friend on the shoulder, and he woke up, slightly irritated. Salvo sat on the opposite side of his compadre Torán, and began to speak:

"Compaí, do you remember what happened last night?" -he asked.

"I don't know, kind of yes and kind of no." -Torán replied.

---

20. De la palma: Political party PNP of P.R. Its symbol is a palm tree.

21. De la pava: Political party PPD of P. R. Its symbol is a dried leaf hat called "pava".

"What do you mean, yes or no? It's either yes or no."

"I don't remember much."

"And what do you remember?"

"I remember we were playing dominoes and pool."

"And?"

"That we drank a lot for free all night."

"And what else?"

"I don't know, but that's not important; what's important is what I have to tell you."

"What do you have to tell me?"

"Compaí Salvo, you know you're like a brother to me, and I don't know why, but I feel like I've hurt you, and before I go, I want you to forgive me, and I want you to know that I love you like an <u>hermano del alma</u>[22]."

Upon hearing these words, Salvo was taken aback because his friend was never one to apologize for anything, let alone express feelings to anyone. If there was one thing he knew about him, it was that he had never gotten married for that exact reason of not knowing how to express his feelings. And even though he didn't lack women's companionship, he was still alone at forty-five.

"Compaí, are you feeling alright?" -Salvo asked, worrying about his friend.

"Better than I have in years." -Torán replied with sincerity.

"And what's the reason for this confession?"

"I don't know; I'm not sure. Still, I have something to ask you before I go."

"And where the hell are you going?"

"I don't know; I'm not sure."

"Compaí, are you messing with me, or there is something wrong with you that you don't want to tell me?"

---

22. hermano del alma: Soul Brother

"I have something to ask you."

"And what is it that you're going to ask me?"

"Compaí, I want you to stop drinking, clean yourself up a bit, and seek God."

Upon hearing this, Salvo burst into uncontrollable laughter because now he was sure that his friend was mocking him. And as he gazed at his friend, he noticed that he looked serious and emotionless. He realized that his compadre wasn't being sarcastic after all, which made him stop laughing.

"Are you serious?" -Salvo asked.

"Yes, that's what I want to ask you." -Torán replied.

"But compaí, you and I know that's the only thing both of us know how to do."

"Even so, you need a change in your life."

"You and me compadre?"

"I don't know; I'm not sure I can change at this point."

"So, I can't drink, but you can?"

"Not really; I just think you should stop drinking and try to make a better life for yourself."

"And is that the only thing you remember from yesterday?"

"I don't remember anything. And what am I supposed to remember?"

"Nothing, compaí, nothing."

The eggs started to sizzle inside the pot as they boiled, and upon hearing this, Salvo found an excuse to leave his friend alone at the table once again and reconsider whether it was wise or not to remind him of how the previous night had ended. As far as he vaguely remembered, the two of them had left the barra with their arms around each other. Not out of affection, but out of the need to support each other's balance. They walked swaying and singing songs they had heard on the vellonera. Once again, they started talking about women and their luck with them.

"Compaí, tell me, who is that woman you say broke your heart?" -Salvo asked.

"One of many." -Torán replied.

"And does she have a name?"

"Yes, but that doesn't matter."

"Come on, compai, who the hell are we talking about?"

"That doesn't matter."

"And is it such a secret that you can't tell me?"

"It's just that you're not going to like it."

"It's not one of my sisters, is it?"

"No, no compai, yo respeto[23]."

"Then who the hell are we talking about?"

"Promise me you won't get mad, and I'll tell you."

"Okay."

"Do you promise?"

"Yes, I promise."

"Okay, well, it was Francisca."

"Francisca, Don Lolo's daughter?"

"Yes, the same one."

"Compadre, you're a real hijo de puta[24]. You knew she was the woman I liked, and you didn't seem to care about her."

"I know, but she didn't like you like that."

"Don't be a pendejo,[25] you know I was trying everything."

"Forgive me, compadre, that's just how life is."

---

23. yo respeto: I'm respectful.

24. Hijo de puta: son of a bitch.

25. Pendejo: asshole

A spark of anger flared within Salvo, and he fell silent, in the haze of drunkenness, his mind couldn't stop thinking about his friend as before. From that moment on, he was a traitor who didn't even respect his own mother. That's how he began to fill with anger and analyze how many times his friend had let him down in that long relationship. Nevertheless, he didn't take a moment to consider what his friend had said about the woman of his dreams. Deep down, he knew it was true that she would never have looked at him as a companion, not even as a friend. This realization hurt Salvo's drunken pride because, despite everything, he was a good and decent man.

Salvo paused momentarily, this time aiming all his false pride and hatred at his compadre.

"You're a cabrón[26]*, a worthless hijo de puta."* -Salvo shouted at his friend.

"Compaí, what happened? Why are you acting like this?" -Torán asked surprised by his friend's reaction.

"You knew that I wanted with that woman, you knew, you miserable hijo de puta."

"Calm down, compaí, you're too drunk to know what you're saying."

"I'm just encojonao...[27] *"* -Salvo hollered.

Out of the blue, he threw a punch at his compadre, and as the latter dodged it, both men fell to the ground because neither could stand on their own. Now on the ground, Salvo turned around to face his friend and tried to hit him, but with so much alcohol in his body, every punch he threw seemed to travel in slow motion and had no physical effect. The two men were making a fool of themselves in the middle of the dirt trail, one throwing punches and the other trying to dodge them. After a few minutes of wrestling, Salvo unleashed his anger; he got up from the ground, and his friend did the same. He stared at him with deep disappointment in his eyes.

"I don't want to have anything to do with you anymore." -Salvo said looking at his friend in the eyes.

"But compadre." -pleaded Torán.

---

26. Cabrón: Asshole

27. Encojonao: slang for pissed off.

Once more, rage filled Salvo with hatred. He roughly pushed his friend away, turned around, and staggered about the road on his way back home. He arrived at his humble home, undressed sluggishly, and went to sleep. The following day, while Torán waited for him at the kitchen table, the events of the previous night vacillated in his mind between reality and imagination, and he couldn't accurately determine to which of these two realms those memories belonged. Then, Salvo had decided that if his friend didn't remember the incident and he himself wasn't sure, it was better to remain silent and live with doubt.

Ready to bring the coffee to the table, Salmo relieved himself of the shame of his actions from the previous night, knowing that his friend had forgotten the unfortunate incident that transpired between them. He felt at peace with himself and glad that he hadn't ruined his relationship with his compadre. Just then, someone knocked on the door of the house, which was located next to the kitchen and was the only way in or out of his humble abode. Salvo placed the cups of coffee back on the counter next to the stove and opened the door to find his older brother Juan standing there, looking distressed and sad. Salvo proceeded to ask:

"What's wrong? Why that face?"

"Haven't you heard about what happened last night?" -Juan asked in disbelief.

"Last night? No! what happened?"

"Torán fell off the cliff next to the dirt trail and died."

"What the hell are you saying? Compaí Torán is in my living room, waiting for coffee."

"Are you crazy or drunk? Torán is dead in the quebrada[28] and they're recovering his body right now.

"You're the crazy one, don't mess around with shit like that, it's not right."

"Look brother, after your drunkenness wears off, you're going to regret it."

"Don't be an idiot, come in and see that Torán is sitting at my table."

Juan and Salvo went to the table where no one was sitting. Salvo was surprised because he knew his door hadn't been opened, and if it had, he

---

28. Quebrada: ravine

would have seen his friend pass him by. Juan left visibly angry, while Salvo went to his room to see if his compadre had gone in there. He didn't see him there, and he even dared to think that his compadre was hiding under the bed, lying among the dust and the urine from the night before. So, he knelt to look under the bed, but no one was there.

Finally, Salvo was filled with doubts and fear that shook his soul. He went to the kitchen, and there were still two cups of coffee, dissipating their warmth and aroma. He sat down again at the small table where he had held that strange conversation with the ghost of his friend, Torán. The shock was so overwhelming that he began to cry out loud, for amidst his thoughts, the surprise and the doubts about what had happened the previous night and that afternoon provided no opportunity for calm. Because the last memory of that tragic night was etched between the reality of the moment and the alcohol of the night. And in that memory, his compadre kept falling backward after a push. Thus, the remnants of death and doubts came to accompany Salvo for the rest of his life; while he continued to ponder whether it was his compadre who should apologize for stealing a love that wasn't his, or if it was he who, through alcohol and false pride, had taken away from his best friend his most precious asset, his life. And there was nothing he could do to explain whether it was alcohol or his conscience that visited him on that fateful morning when he lost his best friend, along with all interest in trying to drink away the realities of his life.

My Life

THAT MORNING, AS I woke up and opened my eyes, I was filled with a sense of wonder and excitement. Everything around me seemed fresh and new, and I felt an absence of worries as I embarked on my journey through the world, brimming with the energy of life. The sun cast its radiant light, guiding my path, although I encountered a few stumbles along the way. But my eagerness to explore was curbed by my parents, who warned me about you, a figure on the horizon. They cautioned me to avoid your presence and advised me to take alternative paths.

However, being ignorant of the fear my parents spoke of, I didn't feel the caution that should have accompanied their words. Without heeding their advice, I continued the path I had chosen in my carefree state. As the morning progressed, I found myself closer to you than I should have been, thanks to my youthful energy and inexperience. I disregarded caution and fear, and I witnessed some friends crossing paths with you, sometimes unwillingly and unable to escape your reach.

As noon approached, my rebellious spirit and the allure of shortcuts took me further away from my parents' guidance. Through the experiences of my morning, I gained a better understanding of you and the reasons for avoiding our encounter. It became clear that no one liked you, and people went to great lengths to avoid you, even if you were near their horizons. Yet, feeling invincible and unbeatable in my own world, I remained indifferent to events that didn't directly concern me. Once again, my parents intervened, reminding me that other people were also important and advising me to pay attention to them before the afternoon arrived, when they might no longer be with me.

As the sun reached its zenith in the sky, and my body overflowed with energy, I continued to immerse myself in complex games where my ideals merged with reality, shaping the beliefs that would guide my steps. I persevered on my journey toward the horizon, where sooner or later, I would have to face you. I expended much energy on seemingly lost causes, but I didn't mind, as my invincibility and vitality felt renewable and everlasting.

The afternoon sun brought weariness to my body, forcing me to recognize that the vigor and energy I had felt earlier in the day were fleeting. I began to grow tired from all the gambling I had indulged in. I decided to sit down and contemplate the reasons behind my weariness. My parents, their faces showing signs of fatigue, continued to offer advice, and I felt grateful that they were still there for me, unlike some of my friends whose parents had already gone to sleep. As the afternoon shadows lengthened, a chill settled in, adding a touch of discomfort to my bones. On the horizon, the descending sun revealed your figure more clearly than before, and a premonition of inevitability began to consume my time and being. My strength waned, and I resigned myself to the idea of meeting you. My steps became slow and unsteady, causing me to stumble more frequently, as the lights of my morning and noon faded into the evening shadows.

Eventually, the night arrived, enveloping me in a comforting aura of reflection. In that moment, my thoughts revolved around you and the eventual encounter that awaited us. Fear was absent, for I had dedicated an entire day to preparing myself to behold your countenance. With my parents already asleep, their counsel remained unspoken. Lying in bed, I contemplated the winding path and arduous journey that had led me to this point. I reminisced about both my triumphs and failures, the scars of setbacks endured, and the profound joys experienced during fleeting moments. I observed children, their exuberant morning energies mirroring my own, and I allowed myself to reflect. The darkness of the night assumed a serene quality, granting respite as I knew that when slumber finally embraced me, there would be no need for further haste. It was then that my horizon merged with yours. Summoning the courage to gaze upon your face, I comprehended that, at last, your embrace would envelop my weary body, finalizing the period of time that others will refer to as... my life.

Thoughts

I am eternally grateful to my father Felix Adorno and my grandmother Antonia Ramos.

THE SANDS OF TIME

for my mom

ON THE SHORES OF the sea, I sat down to gaze at the horizon, searching for a fixed point to focus my thoughts, and all I observed was solitude. I found no sign of what I should do now. The sand beneath my body felt damp and unstable, lacking the firmness needed to take confident steps forward without the possibility of slipping and falling defeated to the ground. I looked down and saw another drop of salty water falling from my eyes, adding a bit more salt to that endless expanse of sand, as endless as your absence in my life. The immensity of the ocean distracted me for a moment. Its grandeur made me feel insignificant in my suffering. Ironically, that very immensity had made me feel alive and full of hope for the future, as happened in the past when our story began. Now, it caused doubts along the solitary path I must continue without you. The waves came and went, in their eternal indecision of whether to arrive or retreat. Some crashed against the rocks, releasing their final breath of life there, reminding me that eventually everything reaches its end along the road. Finally, I rested my head on the sands, and beneath my hair, they felt slightly drier, a little firmer. Once again, I felt your memory attack me in that moment, and I let out my tears filled with the pain of having lost you. And I felt them trickle down my cheeks toward the ground where, just like you, they will be lost forever among the sands of time.

WHO WILL COME FOR ME?

AT CERTAIN MOMENTS IN my life, I have found myself lost in whimsical, crazy, or fantastical thoughts more than once. They consume me in moments when I think about the day my life becomes a story that others tell about me. That day when my tired body and spirit separate from each other, it is then, that I allow myself to imagine how the transition to the other side of time is made. Is there a line of spirits seeking separate and uncertain destinations, or is it a blink of an eye? Could it be that souls disperse in the sands of time without any conception of it? Is it possible that a special messenger would come to fetch us and transport us to the place of our eternal rest? It is in those moments that I also ask myself, "Who will come for me?"

Will it be my grandfather with his usual attire of long pants cut above the ankles and tied with a strip, wearing a faded guayabera[1] and still chewing his tabaco de hoja[2]? Will he show up to fetch me, so that with his deep gaze, he can calm my anxieties about no longer being with my family and friends? Will he be my guide to the afterlife? Bringing me final rest with his essence of peace and dignity acquired through the 95 years he walked this earth. Will he give me advice as he did before? To help me rest in peace, just the same he helped me live in peace. Will he send me on an errand to the

---

1. Guayabera: lightweight man's shirt with pockets and sometimes tucks or embroidery, worn outside trousers.

2. Tabaco de hoja: chewing tobacco

pulperia?[3] So, that on the way to fulfilling one of the many favors he asked of me in life, I can contemplate the process that begins with death.

Or will it be my grandmother who will bring me the news of the moment? Still dressed in her floral dress and a pañuelo[4] on her head, still wearing the glasses she used to wear. So that on the path that leads from life to death, we can talk about her life and the mysteries to which I never had answers, because I lost her at such an early age. Will she answer my questions of who, how, when, where, and why? About the events that occurred in her life long before mine began. Will she free my soul from doubts during this transition that we will all reach someday? Or will she take me to her eternal home where there will surely be a fogón[5] cooking delicious meals as only she knew how. And so, with the són[6] of <u>arroz con gandulez</u>[7], pasteles[8], and <u>arroz con dulce</u>[9], she will bring relaxation to my soul shortly after I have left my body. Will the smoky flavor of the food cooked on the fogón be like an analgesic that soothes the nerves in a disembodied soul?

Will that friend come for me? The one I lost at a very young age. Will he come riding his motorcycle, demonstrating the stubbornness and abandon with which he lived his life? Will he tell me how fortunate I have been, for my life was not cut short; and I was able to see my children grow up, teaching their children what I taught them. Will he speak of how lucky I was to see my skin age and see my gaze become profound over the years and lived experiences? Will he point out a new generation carrying the legacy of what I taught? Or will this friend invite me to go fishing again? And throughout the course of this expedition, will we discuss the anxieties of inexperience in which we find ourselves again? All the same, as in the past we might discuss expectations of life, dreams of youth, and uncertain futures when our lives were just beginning in the past, and we both enjoyed the same things.

---

3. Pulperia: bodega, corner store

4. Pañuelo: handkerchief.

5. Fogón: wood stove

6. Són: rhythm

7. arroz con gandulez: yellow rice cooked mixed with pigeon peas.

8. Pasteles: Puerto Rican version of a tamale, made with mashed green banana, seasoning and meets.

9. Arroz con dulce: delicacy made with sweetened rice with sugars and spices such as cinnamon.

Finally, I wonder, will my parents come for me? Will my father give me examples of how to die with dignity? Will my mother guide my first steps in every facet of my death, just as she did with my life? Will my father teach me again the value of my actions and the importance of doing things correctly? Will my mother speak to me about respect and honesty? Will my parents teach me to be what I am, for they have already taught me to be what I was? And so many times I ask myself, "Who will come for me?"

And I insist that if I could choose that messenger, here and now, I would choose my father; since the day he departed the void he left in me has been impossible to fill. And today, I know that I live the way he showed me to be, and that a large part of who I am is what he was. And I know that if on that day he comes for me, his presence alone will be enough to calm my anxieties, in the moment of my bittersweet end. The memories of his examples to persevere and fight without giving up, will be sufficient to carry me on in death, with the same calmness with which I bid farewell to him. It will serve me once again to analyze the steps to follow on unknown paths as he taught me. If he comes for me, I only know that, although it will hurt to say goodbye to my loved ones, I will do it with the same calmness as the day I had to say goodbye to him. If my father comes to fetch me, I know I have reached the true paradise, because it would only be called paradise if all the beings you love in life accompany you in the eternal rest of death. It is in that way, and only in that way, that when people stand in front of my lifeless body and say, "May he rest in peace," my soul will be filled with joy, because I am embarking on that eternal rest as I did in life, hand in hand with my father...

Because of You

For my father

Viejo[1] since the day you departed from this world, you did not leave my life. I cannot say that I will always remember you because that would be a lie. You cannot remember what is present all the time. Anyhow, regardless of your physical state, your presence always lives in me. I am a direct reflection of what you taught me to be. If I am fair, it's because of you. If I pause to analyze what I should do in difficult situations, it's because of you. If I never find a way to give up without fighting, it's because you're the one fighting along with me, and if I can treat every person with due respect, it's because of you. When injustices bother me and I lose control of my emotions, it's because of you. When I laugh at situations that anger others, it's because of you. And when the voice of my conscience attacks me, making me feel ashamed of having done something unjust or of giving up without trying, it's because of you. There's no need to say that I will remember you, because you will never cease to be present in me in my actions and in the way you taught me to live. You are the voice of my conscience. I will never stop teaching my children what you taught me. And even though you are no longer with me physically, as long as I breathe and have life, your memory, and your teachings will not die. Even though I can admit to myself that I cannot always remember the presence of you who lives within me, if I seek to mirror a voice of reason guided by conscious self-reflection and practical insight, it's because of you.

---

1. Viejo: my old man

The Emptiness of Your Presence

ONE MORNING I WOKE up, like any other morning before in my life. Nothing grand defined that moment of my existence; nevertheless, a sense of melancholy invaded my entire body, filling me with an emptiness that could not be filled with any earthly or spiritual nourishment. This strange feeling of complete emptiness led me in front of a mirror to look at my image, and to make sure that I was physically okay. As I lifted my face and looked directly at the reflection that stared back at me, I could confirm that what weighed me down was the emptiness of your presence in my life; your dear presence in everything that composed the sum of the parts of the person looking back at me in my reflection.

Notwithstanding, my grief was consoled by memories of you which filled my mind with cheerful thoughts, pride, and satisfaction as I realized that my convictions, my notions of what is right or wrong, are a direct reflection of what you taught me over the years, without saying many words. Your examples were my best teachers. Without ever having read a book about how to be a good man, a good human being, or a good father, you were all that and more to me, as well as to other human beings with whom you shared your most precious resource -- your time. You never sat down to tell me how an honest, hardworking, and decent person behaves; you demonstrated it through your actions. You avoided lofty sermons that seek only to teach someone with empty words rather than with real actions. In the constant movement of our lives, there was never a moment of resignation in the face of difficulties, but rather a resolution to constantly fight and never abandon the ongoing battle that is our daily life. That battle was more difficult for you than for me because you made sure that my reality did not repeat the history that initiated the arduous paths that you had to travel in your life.

Once again, nostalgia, sadness, and desolation overwhelmed me as I envisioned the absence of your physical presence in my life, which disappeared on a random night when death came to define the path of your life. The pain caused by the emptiness of your presence was so intense that I couldn't define why. Is it important to remember you, despite the deep pain? Perhaps, it's better to forget, but what does that imply? Would this notion lead me to deny your lived experiences that unearth lessons from your life to guide me in the present? Or would it lead me to erase your legacy and dishonor your memory that unearths lessons from the past that encourages me to ask uncomfortable questions and confront uncertain futures. This nostalgia made me look in the mirror to confirm that the warmth running down my cheeks, was from the tears through which my eyes released the pain in my soul upon realizing that I would never hear your voice again. This is how sadness sometimes clouds the important things in our souls, the only things that can be carried forever. A good example is the affection, and the human warmth that separates the essential from the ordinary. Desolation becomes a burden that you only get rid of if you've had someone prepare you to overcome it and send it to oblivion where it belongs.

Finally, as I bid farewell to my reflection, a sweet realization came: the emptiness of your presence was not a reason to be sad, desolate, or nostalgic. That emptiness was there to help me live. To remind me that in moments when life becomes difficult, giving up is not a real option. It's there to guide how I present to others the person you taught me to be and how I would want my children and my children's children to present themselves to others in the future. That emptiness is there to show me that some things we lose in life have no replacement. That emptiness of your presence, since the moment you physically left my life, has been left to me as a gift from you as a final lesson to my soul: appreciate what you have; enjoy your time; and pass on the opportunities that were offered to you. One last time, I gaze at my reflection before saying goodbye to it. At that moment, I realized that sadness and tears have given way to relief, to the bittersweet joy that comes from remembering what you have lost, with the love and affection that it deserves, despite the pain. It was that bittersweet joy that made me realize that the emptiness I have been feeling since your departure remains there because a big part of you will always be present in my life woven in the essence of my soul.

Eternal Trails

T HAT MORNING FELT PERFECT, the breeze in the plains of that field refreshed the body with the moisture of the morning dew that spread among the flowers. Through that plain walked the woman. She was beautiful and of Taíno[1] complexion, a living representation of her native heritage; of medium height, with a tawny complexion and waist-length black hair, swaying in the humid wind that touched her young body, with the same dew that moistened the flowers. The sun shining on the horizon provided her with the warmth of life. The red roses, yellow ones, and all the other wildflowers knelt at her passage as a sign of reverence to the presence of her physical and spiritual beauty. In the distance, the pitirres[2] and other birds could be heard singing praises of admiration, with the coquis[3] serving as their chorus, for the presence of that woman filled the plains among the mountains with peace and happiness. Along the way, some envious crows tried to make her journey to the horizon more difficult. Nevertheless, the woman persevered, without doubting her resolution to reach her destination. She did not allow herself to be stained by false pride or empty hatred, thus preserving her beautiful essence, which overflowed from her body and shared itself with all those she encountered along her path.

---

1. Taíno: Indigenous people of Puerto Rico

2. Pitirres: (Tyrannus dominicensis) one of the best-known birds in Puerto Rico.

3. Coquí: Species of frog that can only survive in Puerto Rico.,

From atop the hill, her angelic stride left any observer in a spiritual trance that they couldn't explain. The woman looked in all directions with a smile on her lips, through which she let out her immense joy for life in the form of a song. Along that path, every plant she touched with her fingers bloomed almost instantly, giving the world many of the flowers she had nurtured. Her journey to the sublime horizon, in every sense of the word, produced a peace and resignation that few people possess. At the mountaintop, her most coveted angels gathered to watch her walk through that valley of life one last time. The woman looked up and smiled in a manner befitting herself. Even knowing that the path she was taking led to eternal realms, she smiled and raised her hands to bid farewell to her fallen angels. Each imperfect in its own way, yet each equally important to her. And so, that morning, the beautiful woman disappeared into the horizon, leaving behind a valley full of flowers that, although different in color and class, shared the essence of the woman who had nurtured them with love, generosity, and compassion, as well as determination and strength of will. In a sublime instant, the woman vanished into the horizon, leaving a great void while also leaving a great example of life.

That is how I prefer to remember my grandmother's life, for that is how her last days should have been. And though it was not here that she walked through that valley, I know that in her eternal rest, there is such a valley where she will be eternally happy, and the valley will be eternally beautiful, for my grandmother will water all the flowers of eternity with her beautiful presence and her great love.

Autobiography

I was born in the Rio Piedras Medical Center in San Juan, Puerto Rico in the seventies, but I am from a rural neighborhood in Trujillo Alto. I come from a poor family, and I attended the public schools in the town. My first school was the José Julián Acosta Elementary School (now closed). My second school was the Second Unit Rafael Cordero (now closed), and my high school was the Vocational Miguel Such. After completing high school, I moved to New York, where I attended two colleges within the City University of New York (CUNY) system and completed my university studies.

During my childhood, I worked on various things, such as collecting aluminum cans with my father throughout the neighborhood and adjacent areas. Too, I learned how to fish to sell fried fish, and sometimes my father and I also sold coconut sweets, alcapurrias[1], and other fried foods to survive. For a while, there was no drinking water in the neighborhood, which forced us to go and bathe in a spring well next to our humble house. In the 1980s, my father, my older brother Félix, and I worked to expand the house, which was very small, using the assistance

---

1. Alcapurrias: Puerto Rican fritter made with green bananas, seasoning, and meats.

provided by the municipality for low-income families. Thus, I also learned a bit about construction to fend for myself. Throughout all those years, nothing was easy, but nothing was insurmountable either. The examples set by my parents, became valuable lessons that shaped the person I am today, a hardworking man. Not once, I heard my father complaining about the situation. As an adult, I understand that he was a proud man with unbending principles who kept silent about everything that caused him concern or pain with a dignity that few people possess today. Although this was part of my childhood, I am not ashamed of it, nor do I complain about anything because I learned from my father that struggle is part of life's journey.

Although I have a university degree now, I don't give it much importance because, to me, a piece of paper doesn't qualify you as a wise and good person. I believe that if I were to prioritize that, I would be disrespecting my parents and grandparents. Throughout my life, I have always treated people with the respect they show me, as I was taught at home. I don't aim to be perfect, and I don't expect others to be perfect either. Personally, I hate etiquette rules, especially the ones that dictate how I should behave. I enjoy laughing at everything, and that's something I learned from my father's family. We didn't have much, but we didn't go around lamenting that others had more than us. My dad, "Felo," was always the person I admired the most, because his tenacity and determination in the face of challenges taught me to live with enthusiasm without constantly looking back and trying to change what cannot be changed. That's why the photo that I include in my books is of him; without his examples of work and struggle, I wouldn't be here writing stories to honor his memory and keep a part of his history alive through these words.

Other Works by the Author

D EAR READER: IF YOU enjoyed this book, I invite you to share your thoughts on social media.

Scan the QR code to see other works by the author

Libros Talanco

Help me reach more people so they can enjoy my stories as well.